SAVAGE SAINTS

LUCAS STONE
BOOK 5

MARK ALLEN

ROUGH
EDGES
PRESS

ALSO BY MARK ALLEN

Lucas Stone/Primal Justice Series

Fury Divine

Bad Samaritan

Killing Creed

Unchained Vengeance

The Assassins Series

The Assassin's Prayer

The Assassin's Betrayal

Reaper Series

Kane: Tooth & Nail (Fear the Reaper Book 1)

Kill Count

This one's for Gerry. Thanks for being my sidekick.

SAVAGE SAINTS

PROLOGUE

THE CLUB BOUNCED off Stone's already bruised ribs with a meaty thud that sent a fresh jolt of pain blasting through his muscular frame. Some of that muscle definition had been lost to poor nutrition and lack of exercise during the six weeks he had spent in this hell-hole, but he had retained enough that nobody would mistake him for being a weakling. His body remained hard, lean, and powerful despite the near-daily abuse it suffered.

"Speak," his torturer growled in Arabic. "Speak and put an end to the pain." Stone didn't know the man's real name and had dubbed him Nadhil, which roughly translated as *bastard*.

Nadhil boasted above-average height for a male in this part of the world, at least as tall as Stone, maybe even an inch or two more. Not a giant, but pretty impressive for a Syrian. His swarthy skin bulged with the kind veiny, oversized musculature that usually came from steroid injections rather than natural workouts. Not that it mattered much; whatever the source of his strength, it hurt like hell when he slammed the wooden baton into Stone's dangling body. It sounded like a butcher pounding out a piece of meat.

Three rapid strikes across the midsection left Stone's punished abs twitching in agony. But he bit down on the hurt, jaw clenched, letting nothing more than a low, involuntary grunt escape his gritted teeth. It would take more than what Nadhil was doing to make him cry out.

Keep swinging that club, you sadistic piece of shit. Someday I'll return the favor.

Stone's wrists were wrapped in rusty chains hanging from a thick metal hook in the ceiling, arms yanked viciously over his head, his entire body raised until only his toes scraped against the ground. His own weight dragged him down, the relentless pull of gravity making it feel like his arms would tear out of their sockets at any moment.

The walls and floor consisted of solid stone, as if the torture chamber had been carved out of some huge rock, pain and suffering its only purpose. The blows and grunts and curses—but never screams, because they hadn't broken him yet, and he would be damned if they ever would—echoed off the unfeeling stone with the sound of violent misery.

He took another blow to the gut, this one from Nadhil's fist rather than the club. A minor blessing, in that it didn't hurt quite as much. But just because it hurt less didn't mean it didn't hurt. Pain piled upon more pain. That had been his life for the last six weeks, with no end in sight.

"Speak!" Nadhil shouted again, spittle flying from his lips hard enough to spackle Stone's face. "Tell me why you American devils are here, in Syria. Tell me what your mission is." He held up a hand, the one not holding the club. "And do not waste your breath and my time by claiming there is no mission. We already know who you work for."

"You don't know shit," Stone growled, using Arabic as well. He wasn't exactly fluent in the language, but good enough to get his point across.

That point earned him another punch, this one to the jaw. Nadhil's hard knuckles felt like little hammers when they landed. The impact rocked Stone's head to the side. He felt a cut open on the inside of his cheek and his mouth flooded with the salty taste of blood. It drooled from the corner of his mouth and dripped onto his bare chest.

Nadhil strolled over to a wooden table positioned against the south wall and surveyed its macabre contents. Instruments of torture covered every square inch, some of them clean and shiny as a surgeon's scalpel, some of them old and rusty as if they had been spilling blood since medieval times. He tossed down the club and picked up a dagger. It looked old, the steel stained with deep orange blotches, the handle wrapped with electrical tape. When he turned and walked back over to Stone, he wore a sadistic smile that curved like a scimitar across his bearded face. The bastard clearly enjoyed his work.

"You think we know nothing, you filthy American dog. But the truth is, we know everything. You have no secrets from us."

Despite the pain setting his nerves on fire, Stone let out a laugh, a harsh braying sound that sprayed bloody spittle. "Yeah, right, asshole. That's why you keep dragging me in here, hanging me from chains, and asking the same damn questions over and over. Because you know everything."

Nadhil jabbed the tip of the blade into Stone's flesh, just above his navel, letting the steel penetrate a half inch or so. Then he gave it a little twist. Blood oozed out like thick, red syrup. He was so battered and bruised that the pain from the knife barely registered.

"You came here, to this country, to our country, to *my* country, to kill someone, yes?" Nadhil nodded as if answering his own question. "That is what you do, that is who you are. You and your friend back in the cell are assassins. This we know, this we have confirmed."

Stone knew the son of a bitch was lying. There was no way their captors could have confirmed the reason he and Braxx had infiltrated Syria. But he let the guy keep talking. As long as the bastard was running his mouth, Stone wasn't being beaten, or stabbed, or hooked up to battery cables, or waterboarded, or any of the other dozens of interrogation tricks he'd suffered since getting captured.

"So, the only question that remains," Nadhil continued, "is who was your target and why were you sent here to kill them?"

"That's two questions." Stone couldn't help himself.

He earned himself another punch that damn near broke his jaw.

Had that one coming, he thought.

Nadhil's dark eyes narrowed to menacing slits that glittered with anger. "You have a tongue that is sharp and wicked, you son of a whore. Perhaps I should cut it from your mouth and feed it to the dogs."

Stone decided silence was the wise choice right now. Any further provocation and this asshole would do just that.

"But no," Nadhil continued. "No, I think not even that would break you. You would rather choke on your own blood than tell me what I wish to know. I must confess, American, your spirit is strong and difficult to break." He pulled the knife out. The blood flowed a little more freely from the wound, trickling down into the waistband of the thin, dirty, draw-string cotton pants Stone wore. "I think a new approach is required to get the information I need from you."

"I'm not telling you jack shit," Stone said. "Do your worst."

"I *am* going to do my worst," Nadhil replied. "But not to you."

Stone glared at him. He didn't bother asking for an explanation because he knew one would be forthcoming. Nadhil loved the sound of his own voice.

"Tomorrow," the torturer said, "you will hang here once again. But this time, your friend will be hanging beside you. I will ask you questions and if you refuse to answer, I will do terrible things to your friend while you watch. And I do mean *terrible* things. I will scalp the flesh from his skull. I will gouge out his eyes and cut off his nose and use pliers to rip his tongue out by the root. I will sever his cock and sodomize him with his own manhood. Do you understand?"

"You paint a vivid picture," Stone said. "I'll give you that."

"Think about it, you pathetic dog. Tomorrow you will have a difficult decision to make. Tell me what I want to know or watch your friend suffer."

———

After being lowered from the chain and dragged out of the torture chamber, the guards threw Stone back into a small, cramped cell that smelled like stale urine, rotting feces, and unwashed bodies. The other person in the cell rose from a thin, filthy mattress on the floor next to a slop bucket as the steel door slammed shut and the lock secured. "You okay, man?"

Gerry "G-Man" Braxx was a short, stocky, fireplug of a man, but that stockiness came from pure muscle, not fat. He carried the weight well, evenly distributed, and was lighter on his feet than most people expected, due in no small part to his martial arts training. He usually kept his head clean shaven, but six weeks in this Syrian shithole without access to a razor meant his dark blond hair had bristled all over his head.

The same head that asshole plans on scalping tomorrow, Stone thought as he sank down onto his own mattress. Better than sitting on the concrete floor but the difference was marginal. He pulled his knees up toward his chest and rested his elbows on them. "I'll live," he replied. "Wasn't too bad today. A little beating, a little clubbing, some weak-ass knife work. Nothing I can't handle." Stone grinned, though it felt a little tired around the edges. "Wake me up when they get serious about this interrogation."

"You're a tough son of a bitch, no doubt about it. But you can't hold out forever, brother, and there ain't no cavalry coming to save our asses." Braxx sounded pissed, resigned, and bitter, all at the same time.

"That's what expendable means," Stone said. "We knew what we were signing up for."

"'Disavowed' just sounds like a word until it's applied to your ass," Braxx muttered.

"Thought you were some kind of badass Bible thumper," Stone said, checking the knife wound he'd sustained to make sure it wasn't deeper than it initially seemed, followed by a check of his ribs to make sure none of them were broken. Some of those blows from the club had landed pretty hard, but nothing seemed fractured. "Where's your faith?"

"Faith don't make things less painful. Faith doesn't make the hurt go away."

"So why bother with it then? What's the point if the saints suffer just as much as the sinners?"

"Don't be a heathen, Stone."

"Sorry. I'll send out some thoughts and prayers. That better?"

"God, I hate you sometimes."

"You're gonna hate me more tomorrow unless I spill my guts about our target in Syria," Stone said. He quickly recapped Nadhil's sadistic threats, sparing no detail. Braxx needed to know exactly what they would be up against in the morning.

Braxx listened solemnly, thought about it for all of three seconds, and then nodded. "You know what you have to do, right?" Without waiting for an answer, he said, "If it comes down to that, you give them nothing, zip, zero. You hear me? They get fuck-all from us. Not one damn thing. Let the son of a bitch chop me into pieces if that's what it takes, but they don't get to win."

"There's no 'if,'" Stone replied. "You know he's going to do it tomorrow, every last bit of it. The bastard's not big on bluffing."

Braxx shuffled closer to Stone and lowered his voice so that what he said next couldn't be heard outside the cell door. "Yeah, well, maybe we're not here tomorrow."

"You know something I don't?"

"Yes, but let's not get into our sexual prowess right now."

Stone couldn't help but grin. Braxx's steady sense of humor and off-color quips had kept his spirit from getting crushed on more than one occasion during the last six weeks. "You're such a dick," he said.

"Yeah, a big one."

"Are you gonna let me know what you know or not?"

"Yeah, yeah, I'm getting to it. Hold your fucking horses. You got somewhere to be?"

"Anywhere but here would be nice."

"Then you—we—may be in luck," Braxx said. "Overheard some of the other prisoners saying that the Islamic State is going to attack this place tomorrow morning and try to break their buddies out. If that happens, it'll give us a chance to get the fuck outta here too."

Stone digested this information. It was unreliable as hell, nothing more than whispered rumors among prisoners desperately looking for a thread of hope, but it was better than nothing. After a few moments he said, "You and I might very well be dangling from the ceiling when the shit hits the fan. Hard to make a run for it when you're hanging in chains."

"Fear not, Kemosabe, I've got it covered."

"Yeah? What's your plan?"

Braxx winked. "I'm gonna slit my wrists."

———

The night passed slow, the hours long and sluggish. Stone's aching, beaten body refused to let him sleep much, even though he was used to the pain by now. When he did finally manage to slip into fitful slumber, his dreams were dark and bloody and bloated with nightmarish imagery in which his wife and daughter stood over the casket at his funeral. Thick, writhing maggots boiled out from beneath the bulging lid and spilled onto the floor like a seething carpet of corpse-white rice.

He jerked awake with a start and sensed, rather than saw, Braxx staring at him in the dark. He swiped a hand across his forehead, brushing away the cold sweat beaded there.

"You okay, bro?" Braxx asked.

"Yeah, I'm fine," Stone replied. "Just a bad dream, is all."

"Want me to sing you a lullaby, put you back to sleep?"

Stone remained serious. "Thinking about Theresa and Jasmine. Starting to feel like I might not make it back to them."

"Don't say crap like that," Braxx said. "We're busting out of here tomorrow and making our way back home."

Stone knew his buddy was just trying to help, but he couldn't let go of the pensive melancholy that gripped him. "You've got more faith than I do, man."

"I've got faith enough for the both of us," Braxx replied. "I believe God is good and this is the last night we spend in this miserable shithole."

"I thought the Islamic State rebels were getting us out of here, not God."

"Yeah, well, sometimes God uses bad people to get good things done."

Stone lapsed into silence. He could feel depression creeping around the edges of his emotions like a dark, hope-sucking demon and did his best to fight it. He admired Braxx's relentless faith, but he considered himself more of a cynical, agnostic realist. It would take a miracle for them to survive the tortures Nadhil had planned for them when the sun came up, and after six weeks of pain and torment, it was damn hard to believe a miracle was going to show up at the last minute.

Braxx could put his faith in God.

Stone was preparing to meet Him.

———

For some reason, the chains wrapped around his wrists didn't hurt as much this morning. Not because they were any looser than usual—they were not—but probably because he was resigned to his imminent death. The pain seemed easier to bear knowing that it would soon be over, that this day would be his last. Nadhil would threaten Braxx, Stone would hold out as long as he could but eventually cough up the information, and they would both be killed, dragged out into the desert, and left for the scavengers to feed on their rotting flesh.

Braxx hung beside him, dangling from his own chains a few feet away. He seemed far more chipper than Stone, something close to a smirk on his lips. Looked like he was determined to go out smiling. Stone wondered if his friend would be able to maintain his devil-may-care attitude once Nadhil started scalping his skull.

The torturer brandished a large knife with a slightly curved blade. While rust stains blotted the steel, the actual edge looked nice and sharp, glinting in the light of the two bare bulbs that illuminated the interrogation room. Nadhil's evil grin looked just as sharp and metallic.

"Here we are again," Nadhil said. "The day is young but there is much to do. Let us not waste any more time." He looked at Stone. "I trust you have told your friend what will happen to him if you do not answer my questions?"

"He knows," Stone replied.

"Yeah," Braxx growled. "He filled me in last night. Do your worst, you bastard."

"If it comes to that, you may rest assured I will do my worst," Nadhil said. "But perhaps it will not come to that, and we will be able to avoid unnecessary violence." He fixed his cold, reptilian gaze on Stone. "All you need to do is tell me why you are in Syria. Tell me who you were sent here to kill. Speak the truth and spare your friend considerable pain."

"You keep your mouth shut, Stone," Braxx rasped. "You hear me? Keep it shut like a goddamned bear trap."

Stone returned Nadhil's stare. "You heard the man."

The torturer shook his head in faux sadness, but there was a bloodthirsty glimmer in his dark eyes, and the sadistic smile remained carved like a scimitar slash across his swarthy face. "I will not waste time with more threats. The price for refusing to talk has been made clear to you. Now you—or rather, your friend—will pay that price."

He raised the knife toward Braxx's hairline, moving slowly, prolonging the dread.

Stone swallowed hard and closed his eyes. He couldn't bear to watch. He desperately wished he could plug his ears as well, so he would not have to endure the sickening sound of the rusty blade scraping against skull bone. The last thing Braxx had done before they left the cell that morning was making him promise not to give in easily and Stone intended to keep that promise. But knowing what his friend was about to suffer was almost more than Stone could take. He'd been trained to psychologically handle situations like this, but right now that training wasn't working worth a shit.

"Come on, you fucking clown!" Braxx screamed into Nadhil's face and followed it up with a globule of spit. "You wanna play with me? Huh? Then let's play, asshole!"

Nadhil brushed the saliva off his cheek with a chuckle. He seemed genuinely amused. "You Americans think loud voices and filthy words make you tough. But we shall see how tough you really are when I peel the skin from your skull."

"Real original, jerkweed."

"The method of inducing pain does not need to be original," Nadhil replied. "Just persuasive."

"I'll chew off my own tongue and swallow it before I scream for you, motherfucker."

"We shall see about that. Time to play."

Nadhil pressed forward with the knife. Braxx didn't even turn his head away as the blade sliced into his flesh an inch above his left eye. Blood wept from the wound and spilled down, blinding him with red heat, but his face remained stoic.

Nadhil started to drag the knife sideways to make the circular scalping cut.

I can't let this happen, Stone thought. *Sorry, buddy, but I can't just sit here and watch this rotten son of a bitch skin your skull.*

He opened his mouth to tell the torturer what he wanted to hear.

But before he could utter the words, an explosion shook the room.

Dust drifted down from the ceiling, motes dancing erratically in the harsh yellow light from the bare bulbs that illuminated the room. Stone felt the vibrations from the shockwave travel through the chains, down his arms, and tremble through his entire body.

Outside, in the aftermath of the explosion, came the sound of people yelling and shouting. Some of them in alarm, some of them in anger, some of them in hope.

"What was that?" Nadhil growled, turning away from Braxx to stare at the door as if it held the answers. "What is happening?" A second later, another explosion thundered through the prison and rattled the walls. Stone thought it sounded like LAW missiles were being used, but he couldn't be sure. The shouting increased, joined by cries of panic, and moments later, the sound of gunfire added to the noise.

Outside the door, someone ran past, yelling in Arabic, "We are under attack!"

Nadhil walked over to the table and angrily threw down the knife. It clanged against all the other metallic torture devices strewn across the surface. "Do not move," he said to his two prisoners. "I shall return, and we will continue our conversation."

"Can't wait," Braxx said, shaking his head back and forth like a wet dog to get the blood out of his eye. "Hurry back. We'll just be hanging around, waiting for you." He grinned at his own joke.

Nadhil scowled and seemed ready to say something but then shook his head as if deciding it wasn't worth it. He exited the room and shut the door behind him, but Stone didn't hear the sound of the lock being engaged.

Braxx noticed the same thing. "Hear that? Or rather, *don't* hear that? Told you God was on our side."

"Or that big bastard just figured he'd be right back, and we weren't going anywhere, so no reason to lock the door," Stone replied.

"You're a faithless fuck, you know that?"

"Maybe I'll have some faith once we make it out of here."

"Working on it."

Stone watched as Braxx ground his wrists against the steel links of the chains that bound him. Last night he had managed to slice them open enough to bleed but not deep enough to cause serious damage. He had let them scab over and now worked to rip those scabs off. They tore away with little pressure and fresh blood ran out, sliding down his arms in bright red rivulets, slickening his skin.

Stone glanced at the door, willing it to stay closed. If Nadhil came back now, they were screwed.

"C'mon, c'mon, c'mon," he muttered. It had been less than a minute since Nadhil left the room, but it felt like they were running out of time, the doomsday numbers rapidly tumbling down toward zero.

Braxx twisted his wrists together, causing more blood to spill out, coating his flesh. He pulled down with a grunt of exertion, teeth gritted against the strain. It took several tries but finally, lubricated by his own blood, one of his wrists slipped free of the chains. The other quickly followed and he collapsed to the floor, knees banging against the hard stone. He stayed down for several seconds, then gathered himself and powered to his feet.

The key to Stone's chains was lying on the table next to all the instruments of torture. Braxx scooped it up and had Stone free in seconds. They each armed themselves with a blade from the table. Judging from all the autofire corking off outside, they were bringing knives to a gunfight, but it was the best they could do right now.

"Come on," Braxx said, heading for the door. As suspected, Nahil had not bothered to lock it when he left the room. It swung open with the creak of rusty hinges. "Let's blow this popsicle stand."

"You don't have to tell me twice," Stone said. "Right behind you."

Outside, chaos reigned. Armed men, presumably the Islamic State attackers, poured through two gaping holes in the wall, undoubtedly caused by the twin explosions. Smoke and dust hung in the air, no breeze to move them, mixing together to form a stifling, choking battle fog.

Through the blown open wall, the desert beckoned, hot and unforgiving and yet shimmering mirage-like with the promise of freedom. They might die out in that burning wasteland, but it would be better than dying here.

Just about *anything* would be better than the hell that waited them here.

Prisoners fought with their captors, making desperate plays for freedom. The guards used their rifles to gun them down and the Islamic State rebels returned the favor, chugging out sustained salvos of auto fire. Bodies spun and spasmed and crashed to the ground, riddled with bullets. Blood sprays gave the smoke and dust a crimson blush.

Inmates rushed toward the two holes in the wall, making a do-or-die break for it. Not everyone succeeded in reaching the goal, but plenty did. The corpses of those who failed littered the sand between the cellblocks and the wall. Their death twitches served as a gruesome reminder of the brutality of the Syrian prison guards. Panicked shouts and agonized screams and ceaseless gunfire created a violent cacophony of confusion and carnage. A savage symphony, the heavy metal music of madness.

"We've gotta get out of here," Braxx said. "This is not the desert vacation my travel agent promised."

Bullets snapped and cracked through the air. Staying hunkered down wasn't an option. Eventually a slug, even a random ricochet, would nail them. The twin holes in the perimeter wall were only fifty meters away, but a whole lot of hot lead crisscrossed that escape route. "Easier said than done," Stone muttered.

"No choice," Braxx replied. "We make a run for it, our asses might end up chopped liver. We stay here, our asses will *definitely* be chopped liver."

"I know. I'll take point. Stay tight on my six."

"God, I thought you'd never ask."

Stone ignored him. Braxx would crack wise even if the devil himself was impaling him with a pitchfork. Stone pushed away from the building, his bare feet digging into the sand, propelling him forward as fast as he could go. He snatched a pistol off a dead soldier as he ran, a Browning Hi-Power, scooping it up on the fly. It felt damn good to have a gun in his hand again after weeks of not being able to fight back.

He kept his eyes fixed on the nearest hole in the wall like a sniper locking the crosshairs on a target. He heard

Braxx right behind him but didn't look back, trusting his friend to keep up. A bullet whipped past an inch in front of his nose, but he ignored the close call and pushed forward.

Just thirty more yards.

Twenty yards.

Ten.

We're gonna make it!

Stone glanced over his shoulder to give Braxx a triumphant grin.

The grin died stillborn.

Nadhil was twenty-five yards away, a snarl on his bearded face, aiming his pistol at Braxx's back.

Stone stopped in his tracks, spinning around fast enough to send sand flying from beneath his heels. As Braxx crashed into him, Stone dropped the knife from his left hand and shoved his friend out of the way while his right hand raised the Browning.

Too late! Too slow!

Nadhil hit the trigger first. The bullet meant for Braxx's spine instead tore through Stone's flank, blowing out chunks of bloody flesh that looked like a ruptured can of wet dog food. Stone felt searing pain and staggered backward but somehow managed to stay on his feet. Rasping a curse through gritted teeth, he bracketed the torturer in his gunsights and fired a half-dozen bullets as fast as he could, slamming the trigger back again and again.

The impacts punched Nadhil backward against the wall of the building as the tightly clustered rounds slammed into his chest. Blood spurted from the holes in his heart and lungs, a far quicker death than the son of a bitch deserved. But now was the time for survival, not vengeance.

Stone felt his legs start to give out, knees shaking as

he resisted the urge to collapse. He wondered if the bullet had ripped open part of his guts. As he buckled, he felt Braxx's arms go around him, holding him up.

"I've got you, buddy."

"Just leave me," Stone muttered. "Get the hell out of here. I'll cover you."

"Luke, you just saved my life," Braxx replied. "There ain't no way on God's green earth that I'm leaving your ass here. Not happening. I'll carry you all the way home if that's what it takes."

He turned out to be a man of his word.

.

ONE

STONE OPENED his eyes and stared up at the ceiling fan above his bed. The wooden blades slowly oscillated as the dream—no, not a dream, a *memory*—started to recede from his brain as slumber gave way to wakefulness.

Not that he could ever really forget what had happened back then. For that matter, he didn't *want* to forget. Some things deserved to be forever remembered. He and Braxx had saved each other's lives back in that Syrian hellhole, both literally and figuratively, and the bond of brotherhood that had been forged in blood during those long, dark weeks continued to this very day.

During their debriefing, they learned that the compound where they had been held had formerly been a black site for the CIA and that once the Company abandoned it, the Syrian military took it over and used it for much the same purpose—holding and interrogating prisoners they did not want to officially acknowledge. That mainly meant Islamic State terrorists, but clearly they had thought it wise to throw some unauthorized American trigger-pullers in there too. Stone and Braxx had requested the place be taken out with a drone strike and reduced to a smoking crater, but they had been ignored. Something about wasting valuable resources on inconsequential targets. The two warriors took comfort in the fact that they had at least killed their primary torturer.

Stone rolled out of bed and headed to the shower. He cranked up the cold to shock himself fully awake before switching to hot water to soothe away the morning aches. He wasn't getting any younger and his body was starting to remind him of that fact on a daily basis.

As the warm rivulets streamed down over his skin, he traced the scar from the bullet he had taken in Syria, the one meant for Braxx. The slug had torn a wicked gash from his side, grazing a rib in the process, but narrowly missed ripping open his intestines. A couple centimeters to the right and he probably wouldn't be around to tell the tale.

There were plenty of other scars, too, his body a tapestry and testimony to all he had seen, all he had done, all he had suffered back in his warrior days. It had all seemed worth it at the time, like he was making a difference by taking the fight to the enemy, keeping the peace by exterminating those who lusted for war and terror. But in retrospect, there was no denying that the years spent in the killing game had taken a toll, extracting a cost both physical and mental.

Braxx had quit after Syria, no longer willing to pay the price, and Stone had not blamed him for even a single second. He had moved to southern Florida, married a lovely, kindhearted woman named Monica, and settled down into domestic life with an ease that Stone envied, as if he had just flicked a switch and turned the old life off. Two sons, a nice two-bedroom condo right on the water with a spectacular view, a fishing boat that nobody knew why he had bought, since he didn't like fishing, and enough money to enjoy his post-warrior existence of sunshine and leisure. God knew he had earned it.

Stone made a mental note to give his old buddy a call. It had been too long. One of them usually jingled the other every six months or so, but they hadn't seen each other in years. In fact, the last time they had been together was at Jasmine's funeral. Despite being a God-fearing man, Braxx had not offered Stone trite, cheap, bumper-sticker platitudes regarding the death of his daughter. He had simply been there, a comfort, a shoulder to cry on. Stone had respected that even back then. Now that he had found God himself, he respected it even more. Braxx's "no bullshit" approach to faith was just one of the many reasons they remained committed friends despite the distance.

Yeah, it was time for a visit with his pal. It had been too damn long. Some south Florida sun and sand would do him good. They could sit on the patio, crack a couple cold ones—Pepsi, since Braxx was a teetotaler—watch the glory of God in the sunset, and talk about whatever the winds of conversation brought their way.

But that was for another day. Right now, he had a meeting scheduled with Father Andy Lillegard over at St. Luke the Beloved Physician Episcopal Church in Saranac Lake.

He dressed quickly, pulling on a pair of jeans and a loose, moisture-wicking t-shirt. It was probably hot enough for shorts—contrary to popular belief, summers in the Adirondack Mountains often saw the temperature shoot well past the 80-degree mark, but Stone was generally a pants guy, preferably denim. It was the cowboy in him. You could take the boy out of Texas, but you couldn't take Texas out of the boy. So heat be damned, he was wearing jeans, boots, and his Stetson with the rattlesnake band.

Out in the kitchen, he whipped up some scrambled eggs, venison sausage patties, an English muffin, and washed it all down with a cup of coffee that was heavy enough on the creamer to call his masculinity into question. This was all done under the watchful eye of Max, his rescue Shottie. The big, lowkey Shepherd/Rottweiler mix with his head all scarred up from his dogfighting days gave him a longsuffering look that seemed to say, *Care to tell me why you get to eat first? Can't you see I'm starving here, man?*

"Look at you," Stone said to his four-legged companion. "Just laying there, wasting away to nothing." He chuckled, tossed him a bite of sausage, and performed the daily morning ritual of scooping kibble into the dog bowl. As Max scarfed down his breakfast, Stone grabbed his keys, climbed into his '78 Blazer, and headed south out of Whisper Falls toward Saranac Lake with AC/DC blasting out the rolled-down windows.

―――――

Forty-five minutes later, Stone and Father Andy were deep into one of their spiritual—and spirited—debates. It was one of their favorite pastimes when they got together.

"Jesus very clearly and without stuttering said to turn the other cheek," Andy said, not for the first time today. "If that's not a stone-cold, bagged-and-tagged, case-closed argument for pacifism, then I don't know what is."

"Christ also told His disciples to go buy swords," Stone countered. "If He was so against violence of any kind, why'd He tell them to do that?"

"You're taking that out of context."

"That's debatable, and you know it."

"Jesus also said that whoever takes up the sword will perish by the sword."

Stone grinned. "That Jesus was quite a complicated guy, huh?"

Stone had met Father Andy last summer at a prayer breakfast hosted by the Adirondack Community Church in Lake Placid, which had seen most of the pastors and clergymen in the tri-lakes area gathered together for food and fellowship. The Episcopalian priest had stuck out like a sore thumb due to his white Stetson, cowboy boots, and a glorious mustache that would have made Kurt Russell as Wyatt Earp in *Tombstone* jealous. As the only two guys sporting Stetsons in the group, they had gravitated toward one another, engaging in conversation and staying in touch after the prayer breakfast.

Their friendship had experienced a few road bumps in the early going, as Andy's more traditional, ritualistic faith rubbed up against Stone's earthy, freewheeling style. But they had quickly come to the realization that they were both men of God just doing their best to live a life of faith. As their respect for one another grew, so did their tolerance for each other's approach to the spiritual journey. They had eventually abandoned any antagonism that may have been present in the beginning and adopted a "live and let live" approach to dealing with their theological differences.

But that didn't mean they didn't argue about them all the time.

"You know He was called the Prince of Peace, right?" Andy asked. "Not the Prince of Ass Whoopin'."

"Yeah, well, the Prince of Peace whipped people and flipped over tables in the temple," Stone replied. "And not just some spur of the moment whipping either. The Bible says Christ 'fashioned a scourge.' Think about that,

Andy—He took the time to go and make a whip. If that's not premeditated violence, I don't know what is."

"Pretty sure we're not supposed to compare Christ's holy anger with the violent impulses of our human nature."

"Spin it any way you want, but it makes it hard for me to believe that Jesus was a pacificist when He took a scourge to people who pissed Him off, however righteous the reason."

Andy rolled his eyes and shook his head but beneath his thick mustache lurked a little grin. "You're such a heathen, Luke. You know that, right? Sometimes I think you've got your heart set on Heaven, but your boots pointed toward Hell."

Stone returned the grin. "Good thing God loves rebels and scoundrels just as much as He loves the saints."

"You got that right." Andy's grin faded, the look on his face turning earnest, his voice becoming somber. "Truth be told, my friend, there are times, many times, when I wish God had not called me to be a pacifist. I love a good debate, and kicking this thing around with you is a fun way to pass some time, but the truth of the matter is, I understand your side, where you're coming from. But that is not the path the Lord has chosen for me."

"Believers are not all called to the same path," Stone said. "We all walk different roads, we all ride different horses, and we're all different tools in God's toolbox. If He's made it clear to you that you are not to raise a hand in violence, then that is the calling you must obey."

"Different tools in God's toolbox." Andy seemed to roll that around in his head and then smiled. "I like that. Might steal it for a sermon title one of these days."

"Not everyone in your congregation will appreciate the message. Too many believers want all Christians to be exact replicas of what they think a Christian should look like, with no room for individuality or different callings. Like we're all a bunch of sanctified clones."

"Well, it's been my experience," Andy said, "that if you're not pissing off some people with your message, then you ain't preaching the truth."

"Amen to that," Stone agreed.

They sat in comfortable silence for a few moments, each pondering their own thoughts, and then Andy switched subjects. "So, Amber and the rest of the missionaries made it to Mexico yesterday without any problems, thank God. They're currently situated at the host church before they head to the first village tomorrow."

"Glad to hear they made it okay," Stone said. He knew St. Luke's had been planning this mission trip to Mexico for several months now. It was something that Amber, Andy's wife, had felt called by God to lead. The goal was to take food, medical supplies, and of course, the gospel message to some of the poor, rural, destitute villages in the region. They had covered the cost through various fundraisers, auctions, and charitable donations—Stone himself had anonymously given a generous amount to ensure the mission happened—and Amber, along with five other volunteers, had flown to El Paso, Texas yesterday where Sacred Impact Mission Group helped ferry them across the border to Holy Spirit Anglican Church on the outskirts of Juarez.

"Feels weird not to be there with them," Andy said.

"They're only gone for a week, right? Couldn't you have tagged along?"

"Sure, I could have," Andy replied. "But this was Amber's idea, her calling. She—we—really felt like the Lord wanted her to lead this missionary group and my presence would have made that more difficult for her, since the others would have kept looking to me, since I'm the priest at the church." He shook his head. "No, it's better for me to sit this one out. It's just hard, being here while she's in another country." He shot Stone a crooked grin. "Doesn't help that I think my secretary has a bit of a crush on me."

"Wendy?" Stone only knew the woman enough to exchange polite pleasantries in passing. "Really, you think so?"

"Just a gut feeling at this point, a vibe I get from her. No hard evidence or anything like that."

"You worried she'll act on it, make some kind of pass while Amber is gone?"

"No, not really." Andy shook his head. "She knows I'm happily married."

"So, you're just worried about Amber, then, whether or not she's safe over there."

Andy shrugged. "Not really. Sacred Impact Mission Group is very reputable, never had any problems, and their support system is top-notch. Besides, you know me —I'm a big believer in that whatever happens, that's how God wanted it."

In the past, Stone had risen to that particular bait, but today he let it go. Part of him wanted to tell Andy that he was looking at the world through the rose-colored glasses of faith, as if evil didn't exist and innocent people didn't suffer cruelty at the hands of outlaws and cutthroats. But he held his tongue, because the reality was, Andy already knew that. He was not a naïve man, nor was he some noodle-spined priest, ignorant of the harsh realities of a fallen world. He just chose to put his absolute trust in God, to believe that whatever happened was in the Lord's hands.

In some ways, Stone admired him for that. That being said, Stone preferred to trust God *and* carry a gun. Faith would take you far, but a little firepower for backup never hurt. Heaven helps those who help themselves and all that shit.

"You're a good man, Andy," Stone said, meaning every word. "And when you get right down to where the horseshoe meets the nail, I think you're a damn sight better believer than I am."

Andy waved away the praise like he was shooing a fly and made a scoffing noise way back in his throat. "Get out of here with that nonsense, man. I may be *different*, but I'm not *better*."

"Fair enough."

Stone hoped Andy never found out just how different they actually were.

TWO

STONE SPENT NEARLY three hours jaw-jacking with Andy—nothing unusual for them; their record was four hours—before heading back to Whisper Falls and stopping by the Birch Bark Diner for lunch. He was in the mood for one of their so-called "garbage plates," which consisted of a pile of french fries topped with two cheeseburger patties and slathered with some secret meat sauce and mustard. Some people finished it off with chopped onions, but Stone would rather eat the asshole out of a dead skunk than eat an onion.

He was also in the mood to see his favorite waitress.

Holly set the giant plate of food in front of him and slid into the booth across from him. She watched with amusement as he shoveled forkfuls into his mouth like a starving man at a feast. "Hungry?" she teased with a twinkle in her pretty blue eyes. "You're acting like you haven't seen food in a week."

"Famished."

"Did you skip breakfast or something?"

"No, I'm just a growing boy."

Holly smirked. "I'll leave that one alone."

Stone shook his head. "Don't be wicked."

Her smirk turned into a chuckle. "What can I say? Sometimes you bring out the best in me, sometimes the worst." She slid out of the booth. "I need to go check on the other tables while you chow down like a horse at a corn trough." She touched him gently on the shoulder before walking away.

Stone watched her go, not for the first time—or even the hundredth—admiring the view. There was no denying that she made a pair of jeans look damn good. Then again, Holly was pretty enough to make just about *anything* look good.

They had a mostly unspoken agreement to keep things in the "good friends" zone rather than becoming romantically entangled, but more and more recently, Stone was realizing that they couldn't remain in that no-man's-land forever. The desire, the attraction between them, was clear as day, rarely acknowledged but rarely unnoticed either.

What are you scared of? an inner voice prodded. *Happiness?*

No, Stone thought. That wasn't it.

What is it then? Scared of getting your heart broken again?

No, that wasn't it either.

He wasn't afraid of getting his heart broken.

He was afraid of breaking hers.

Stone finished eating with a feeling of melancholy. Why did life have to be so damn hard sometimes? Why did emotions have to be so complex?

Holly returned to the booth as he mopped up the last dregs of meat sauce with the final french fry. "Feel better?"

"It hit the spot, yeah." Stone stacked the silverware on the dirty plate.

"You should come over to the house soon, let me cook you some real food."

"Holly, we both know you can't cook for shit," he said with a grin.

She feigned outrage. "You take that back right now, Luke. You know damn well I make a mean peanut butter and jelly sandwich."

"Never let it be said you don't know your way around gourmet cuisine."

"Fine," she said, smiling. "We can do takeout. It'll give you a chance to talk to Lizzy, hear all about her new boyfriend."

Stone leaned back in his seat. "Another one? Isn't this, like, the third guy in six months?"

"Cut her some slack. She's only seventeen. No reason for her to be settling down yet."

"Who's the latest crush?"

"Eric Wegman."

"Any relation to Frank Wegman, the new pastor over at Saranac Lake Baptist Church?"

Holly nodded. "That's his father."

"So, Lizzy is dating a preacher's kid."

"Something wrong with that?"

"Not at all. Those stories about pastor's kids being hell on wheels are mostly wild exaggerations." He paused. "Mostly."

"Eric seems like a good enough guy," Holly said. "I guess he's the drummer for the worship band at the church. They hang out over there a lot while he practices."

"That doesn't bother you?"

"First," Holly replied, "she's seventeen, not seven. Second, I highly doubt that they're going to do it in a church."

"I don't know." Stone feigned seriousness. "You know how those drummer types are."

"Yeah." Holly smiled, reached across the table, and flicked the brim of his Stetson. "Almost as bad as cowboys."

"Harsh," Stone said. "If I had feelings, they'd be hurt."

"Then I guess it's a good thing you're a coldhearted son of a gun."

"Only part of the time. The rest of the time, I'm just a regular son of a gun."

"You're a regular son of a something, that's for sure."

"Well, I'll be a real son of a something if this Eric fella hurts my favorite teenager."

"Well, you can relax. Way things have panned out with the last two boys, Lizzy will be the one doing the heartbreaking, not the other way around. Besides, I told you, he's a good guy, treats her well." She grew serious. "Honestly, Luke, he's been good for her. She doesn't talk about it much—at all, really, at least not with me—but I think she's been struggling with the fact that her father is gone. She never knew him, but he at least *existed*, know what I mean? I'm not sure she knows how to feel now that he's dead and gone."

Stone felt tension creep through him but did his best to hide it from Holly, though she knew him well enough that she could probably sense it, and probably even had a general idea what caused it. Because whatever troubled emotions Lizzy was suffering, Stone bore at least partial responsibility. He had gunned down Lizzy's father after the man broke out of a federal prison and invaded Whisper Falls looking for revenge on the family that he felt had betrayed him. The convict had left a trail of corpses in his wake and had been a heartbeat away from killing Holly when Stone put a bullet in his head.

Afterward, Lizzy had made it clear that she didn't blame him for pulling the trigger, but it had clearly done some psychological damage. How could it not? Lizzy was a tough kid, no doubt about it, but watching your father get his head blown off would take its toll on even the toughest of teenagers.

"Has she changed her mind?" Stone asked, troubled. "Does she think I shouldn't have killed him?"

Holly reached across the table and put her hand over his. It felt warm, comforting, like it belonged there. "No, of course not. She knows you didn't have a choice, and she doesn't blame you, not even a little bit. She just..." Holly hesitated, looking for the right words. "She just feels alone sometimes. I know that doesn't make sense, since her father hadn't been in our lives since she was a little girl but knowing that your dad is dead feels different than knowing that your dad just isn't around."

"She's not alone. She has to know that."

"She's a seventeen-year-old girl. Half the time, they feel alone no matter how many people are around them."

"Yeah, well, what I know about teenage girls could fit in an empty shotgun shell and still have plenty of room for the powder," Stone said. What he did not say was that he never got the chance to learn, since Jasmine had died long before those teenage years hit. But he definitely thought it and immediately had to swallow the lump in his throat.

Holly patted his hand. "Don't worry, we'll teach you everything you need to know."

"I'm counting on it." Stone took out his wallet and threw some money on the table to cover his lunch.

"Before you go," Holly said, "there's something else I think you should know."

"About Lizzy?"

"No, about David White."

Stone inwardly bristled at the name. White was the head deacon at Faith Bible Church and one of those people that made it hard to follow the scriptural command to love your neighbor. He was a legalistic, self-righteous, holier-than-thou prick who took great delight in being a thorn in Stone's side.

He was also madly in love—or at least, delusional infatuation—with Holly, and believed God had promised him that she would be his wife someday.

"What's new with Dave?" Stone asked, trying to not spit the man's name out through clenched teeth like some kind of obscenity.

"Actually, it's nothing new," Holly replied. "It's something old. Your favorite deacon has started hitting on me again."

Stone crumpled his napkin into a ball and tossed it onto the plate and tried not to wish that the napkin was David White's throat. "Much as I'd like to," he said, "you know I can't stop him from asking you out."

"Luke, it's every damn morning these days. He strolls in here with that irritating smile on his face, orders breakfast, then tells me over and over again that God says I'm supposed to be his wife." She let out a longsuffering sigh. "I got so angry with him yesterday that I told him to shut the fuck up or I'd pour hot coffee on his balls."

"Nice." Stone smirked. "What'd he say to that?"

"He actually got all annoyed and told me to stop acting like a Jezebel, whatever that's supposed to mean."

"White's way of calling you a bitch, since he won't use the actual word. Thinks profanity is a sin."

"But he's perfectly fine with sexual harassment? Because that's what he's doing."

"I'll take care of it."

"By 'take care of it,' do you mean you'll knock his teeth down his throat?"

"Probably not." Stone stood up and clamped the Stetson down tighter on his head. "But I wouldn't rule it out."

THREE

STONE FOUND White at the church, unboxing the new hymnals they had ordered, humming an off-key version of *I Have Decided to Follow Jesus*. The head deacon looked up when Stone walked into the sanctuary and his face wrinkled as if he had just sucked all the juice out of a lemon. Both anger and worry flashed in his eyes. No surprise there; Stone had spent a lot of years making people experience those particular emotions.

"I didn't think you were coming in today," White said. "Had I known, I would have waited for another day to do this so our paths wouldn't cross. Figured you would be too busy with sheriff's work to bother actually leading your flock."

Stone ignored the cheap shot and cut right to the chase. "I wasn't planning on coming in," he replied. "But I had a change of heart after having a chat with Holly down at the diner."

White glanced up at the large wooden cross hanging on the wall behind the pulpit as if seeking some kind of divine strength for the confrontation, then sighed heavily and faced Stone. "So, what? You're here to beat me up or something? That the plan?"

"What makes you think that?"

"You're a violent man. Think about it—how many people have you killed since you came to this town?" White started ticking them off on his fingers. "All those survivalists. The drug dealers. The neo-Nazi terrorists. Jack Dawson and all his men." He shook his head. "You must have a body count of over three dozen by now and you've barely been here two years. This place is running red with blood because of you."

"I'm only violent when I have to be." Stone ignored the inner voice that called him a liar. "And as long as you and I come to an understanding, I don't think I'll need to be violent today."

"An understanding about what?"

"Holly Bennett."

White adopted a smug look that Stone wanted to wipe off his face with a sandblaster. "Oh, you mean my future wife."

Stone leaned his hip against the end of a pew and folded his arms across his chest. "That's what I'm talking about, Dave. You've gotta stop with that shit."

"I really wish you wouldn't curse in church. Or at all, for that matter."

"I really don't care what you want," said Stone.

"And I really don't care what you think about me and Holly."

Stone rolled his eyes heavenward and fired off a silent, *Lord, help me.* Aloud, he said, "Get it through your thick skull—there is no you and Holly."

"That's not what God told me. He has made it clear in my prayers that Holly will be my wife someday. Remember what Psalm 37:4 says? 'Delight yourself in the Lord and He will give you the desires of your heart.'"

"You really need to learn the difference between God's voice and your personal delusions."

White made a scoffing noise. "If you think for one single moment that I'll take spiritual advice from someone like you, then you're sorely mistaken."

Stone's eyes narrowed. "Then maybe you'll take a threat from someone like me. You either back off from bothering Holly or I'll remove you as head deacon. I don't give a damn how long you've held the position."

"You can't do that."

"I can and you know it. Cross the line with Holly again and your ass is fired."

White huffed and cocked his head to the side. "You don't see anything wrong with your behavior? You're abusing your pastoral authority to protect a love interest that isn't even a member of this church. Heck, she barely even attends services."

"You can spin it any way you want. But think about how it looks to have the head deacon of our church stalking and harassing a member of the community."

"Oh, right. Because you're one to lecture me about Christlike behavior," White drawled with every last ounce of sarcasm he could muster. "Maybe take the log out of your own eye before you worry about the speck in mine."

Enough of this shit, Stone thought. He'd played nice long enough. He felt his better angels lose control as his warrior side seized the reins. He pushed away from the pew, bunched his fist in the front of White's shirt, and yanked the deacon close. "I'm not *asking* you to leave her alone," he rasped. "I'm *telling* you."

White looked shocked at first, his face going white. But it quickly reddened with anger and defiance. "And if I don't?"

"I'll knock your teeth down your throat."

White's jaw dropped open and his eyes bulged. "You can't talk to me like that!"

"Pretty sure I just did."

"I'll take this before the church, let them know that you threatened me with physical violence." White raised his arm and pointed at Stone's face, jabbing his finger to punctuate his words. "You're finished here, you hear me? You and your cowboy Christianity—if you can even call it that—are done."

"You can take that road if you want," Stone said. "But if we're spilling secrets to the church, I'll tell them how much you've been harassing Holly. I'm willing to bet that by the time I'm done talking, they'll be perfectly fine with the threat I just made. Question is, are you willing to bet they won't be?"

White looked steaming mad, the top half of his ears glowing sunburn-red. "This isn't over, Stone. Not by a long shot."

Stone released the head deacon's shirt and shoved him away. "It damn well better be."

FOUR

HOLY SPIRIT ANGLICAN CHURCH, JUAREZ, MEXICO

THE SIX MEN swarmed the church under the cover of darkness, moving like wraiths in the night, shadows in the shadows, their near-silent shapes as dark as the matte-black weapons they carried. There was no uniformity to the guns; just a mishmash of AKs, FNs, M4s, SCARs, and assorted pistols, mostly Glock or Beretta. All brandished knives on their belts. The man these men called master did not care what they armed themselves with, just as long as whatever weapons they chose were sufficient enough to accomplish the task at hand. Satisfactory completion of the assignment was all that mattered, the only goal they pursued.

If they failed to accomplish their objective, they would not want to return to the compound. The man known as *El Crucificador*—The Crucifier—did not tolerate failure well. When angry, his rage knew no bounds, and he would nail their hides to the cross.

Literally.

The targets were nestled in the recently renovated

dormitory behind the church, just beyond the courtyard, no doubt tucked in for the night after their bedtime prayers. The strike team easily breached the iron gate, snipping off the padlocked chain with a pair of bolt cutters. They quickly crossed the packed earth, maneuvering around stunted, skeletal trees and wilting shrubbery to access the stone pathway that led them to the dormitory door, which they immediately kicked open.

They heard a woman call out, "Who's there?" a moment before they tossed in a couple of flash-bang grenades. If she said anything else, it was drowned out in the 170-decibel thunder of the detonation and the 7-megacandela, pupil-blasting burst of white light.

Instant incapacitation.

The strike team entered the dormitory to find the six American missionaries writhing in pain and confusion on their bunks or on the floor. The two oldest—an elderly married couple, according to the intel they had been given—thrashed around like salted slugs, clutching at their ears as blood leaked from savaged eardrums. With the echoes of the explosions receding, the terrified screams of the victims could be heard. You would have thought they were suffering the *incendios* of hell, the way they were sobbing, crying, and carrying on.

The leader of the team found the noise annoying and shouted at them to shut up. *"Callate!"* Spanish being his native tongue, he used it first, then immediately repeated the command in English, this time adding in some colorful profanities for punctuation.

A woman stepped forward, feet bare, wrapped in a bath robe. Average height and build, dark hair pulled back in a loose ponytail, eyes bright with a volatile mixture of fear, shock, and anger. "What is the meaning of this?" she demanded.

Who does this puta think she is, to talk to me so? the leader thought.

Without warning, he whipped the butt of his SCAR assault rifle across her face, knocking her head to the wide and bruising her jaw. He pulled the blow just enough to avoid breaking bone, knowing that *El Crucificador* would want her intact. He followed up by ramming the rifle into her midsection. Not enough to rupture any internal organs, but enough to let her know who was in charge.

As she tried to double over in pain, he grabbed her ponytail and jerked her head up so hard that he felt some strands of hair tear loose. "Do not speak unless spoken to," he hissed, lips peeled back from his teeth in a feral snarl. "Or else you might lose your tongue."

The shock and anger disappeared from her eyes, leaving behind nothing but fear. Her oval face grew even more pale than it had been.

"Do I make myself clear?" the leader asked.

She nodded as best she could with her hair clutched in his fist.

"*Excelente.*" He let go of her ponytail and shoved her backward. She stumbled away from him, almost tripping over the elderly couple on the floor.

The missionaries were rounded up and flex-cuffed with their hands behind their backs. They were all searched, and any cell phones, money, or jewelry were stuffed into a backpack carried by one of the strike team members. They were not handled gently during the pat-downs and the team leader noticed the woman growing angry again as rough hands groped her.

This bitch has some spirit. We'll have to keep an eye on her. Can't have her riling the others up into some kind of half-assed rebellion.

He briefly considered violating her right then and

there in front of the other missionaries to hammer home the point that, spirit or not, she was not in charge. Maybe even let all the boys take a turn too. But he almost immediately discarded the idea. *El Crucificador* might have plans for her and their master was not a fan of sloppy seconds.

"Listen to me," the leader said, loudly addressing the group. "You are now guests—prisoners or hostages, if you prefer those terms—of Señor Armando Ochoa. You will be blindfolded and moved from this church to a new location where you will be kept safe while arrangements are made for your release."

"You mean ransom," one of the male missionaries— the youngest, according to their intel—said with a harsh edge of bitterness.

The leader smiled but no mirth reached his dark eyes. "I will say to all of you what I said to the *puta* a moment ago: speak without being spoken to and the tongue will be cut out of your mouth." He glared at each missionary individually to make sure they got the message, his heartless gaze zeroing in on each of them like a sniper's crosshairs. "Your compliance during the transport and confinement at Señor Ochoa's compound is not only expected, it is demanded. *Comprende?* Any resistance, any backtalk, any problems from you at all will be met with violence. Do as you are told, do not cause us any trouble, and you will be back home with your families in just a few short days."

A commotion at the dormitory's entrance, where the breached door dangled on a single hinge, caused him to turn around. A member of the strike team came into view, dragging an old priest with him. He dropped him in front of the leader the way you would drop a sack of garbage and said, "Found him sneaking around outside."

The leader smirked. "You the rescue party, padre?"

The priest looked like he was pushing eighty. Long, frizzy, silver-almost-white hair drooped from a liver-spotted scalp down to thin, bony shoulders draped in a black, threadbare cassock. He appeared to be absolutely outraged. "I am Father Benedicto. What in *Dios* name is the meaning of this?" he demanded. His body might have been frail and trembling, but his voice was strong and firm.

"We're escorting your guests to their new accommodations," the leader replied.

"I can't let you do that," said the priest.

"You can't stop us." *Time for a demonstration of power,* the leader thought. The old *el clerigo* had provided him an easy opportunity to show they were not to be fucked with.

He leveled the SCAR, holding it down by his waist, directly in line with the kneeling priest.

The man holding Father Benedicto released him and backed away as the team leader triggered a half-dozen 7.62 mm bullets into the old man's chest. The cassock rippled under the hammering, nearly point-blank impacts and grew wet with blood. The priest raised his head toward heaven and threw his arms out wide in a cruciform pose as chunks of flesh and bone exploded from the exit wounds in his back. He stayed that way for a few moments, even after the gunfire stopped, and then slowly toppled forward, dead before his wrinkled face hit the floor.

The rest of the strike team laughed as if they had just watched a comedy routine instead of a brutal execution. One of them mockingly made the sign of the cross and said, "Rest in pieces, *padre.*"

The woman stared in horror at the gunned-down priest. Father Benedicto had been one of the kindest, gentlest clergymen she had ever met. Tears streamed down her cheeks. "You...you murdered him," she said softly, voice trembling as if she couldn't believe what she had just witnessed. She lifted her weeping eyes to the leader and her voice rose as well. "He was a man of God!"

"Then God should be happy to have him," the leader retorted with a sneer. He turned away, stepped over the still-twitching corpse, and made a circular motion in the air with his finger. "*Rápidamente!* Move them out!"

———

Amber Lillegard sat in the back seat of a moving SUV and tried not to panic, taking deep breaths to keep the desperation at bay. Despite the air-conditioning in the vehicle, sweat dampened her hair and trickled down her face in salty rivulets. It was a cold sweat, the sweat of shock and fear and anguish. Her eyes felt hot, wet, and feverish behind the blindfold.

But the blindfold also gave her hope, however slim and fragile it might be. It meant that maybe she—and the others—were not going to die. If their abductors were just taking them somewhere to kill them, there would be no need for the blindfolds. Maybe, just maybe, there was a chance they would come out of this ordeal alive.

The missionaries had been split up between two black SUVs with dark-tinted windows, three missionaries in each one, with three armed guards riding along. Their hands remained bound and blindfolds had been tied tightly across their eyes. So tight, in fact, that the pressure was giving her a headache, pain spiking through her head. But that was the least of her worries, given the circumstances. She didn't waste breath complaining, because it would not do any good and might result in her tongue getting carved out of her mouth.

The cold-blooded execution of dear old Father Benedicto had proven beyond all doubt that these men—these ruthless, merciless men—meant business and were not prone to idle threats.

Who were they? Some random gang looking to snatch them up and make a quick buck off a ransom demand? A group with a grudge against the church? Members of the Juarez cartel that operated in this area? The latter seemed most likely, given the heavy firepower their captors had employed in the abduction, but Amber could not think of a single reason why a cartel would target them. The team leader had mentioned someone named Armando Ochoa. The name held no significance to her. Who was he and what did he want with them?

Hopefully it would all be explained when they reached their destination, wherever that might be. Ochoa's compound, if the leader had been telling the truth. Until then, she decided to stop thinking about it, to stop letting the confusion ricochet around in her skull like a manic pinball and turn it over to God. She knew He was there, even now, in these dark times, and sought peace and comfort in the knowledge. She squeezed her eyes shut behind the constricting blindfold and turned her anguished thoughts into anguished prayers. She imagined them flying through the roof of the speeding SUV, through space and time, past saints and angels, to the heavenly throne of God Himself.

Beseeching the Lord for strength, comfort, and salvation helped calm her ragged nerves. Her lips moved, forming the words, but she made sure to stay silent, not wanting to annoy her abductors and risk their wrath.

She felt the SUV jostle as it veered off whatever paved highway they had been traveling on and started rumbling over a dirt or gravel road. The vehicle's suspension did its job, but the ride was definitely rougher than before. Clearly, they were being driven away from civilization and that worried her.

Maybe they're taking us out into the desert to put bullets in our heads and leave our bodies for the vultures to feed on.

She immediately shook her head as if to rattle away that gruesome imagery, not wanting to let thoughts of bloody skulls and flesh-stripped bones fester in her mind. She couldn't afford to go down the road of dark thoughts. Hard as it might be, she needed to stay as positive as possible, and not just for her own sake. Like it or not, she was the leader of this missionary group. The others would be looking to her for strength and she would have none to give them if she wallowed in fear and let it consume her like a poison. Given the situation, it was only natural that she felt scared—okay, terrified—but she had to dig deep and find the faith, the inner power, to push through that fear.

Dear God, I need Your help.

Her mind turned to the others who had volunteered to join her on this mission trip. Bill and Claudia Dreyson were a husband-and-wife couple in their midfifties from the Lutheran congregation that shared the sanctuary with St. Luke's. Dianne Fitzgerald, also in her mid-50s, was a substitute teacher at the Saranac Lake High School and oversaw the local food pantry. Gary Gunther was the youngest member of the group, a young man in his early thirties who had recently quit his job as a fishing guide and announced God had called him to the priesthood. The sixth and final member was Jack Spurgeon, a good-looking single guy in his late thirties who seemed more interested in getting a free trip to Mexico than actually doing the Lord's work. Amber had almost nixed him coming along but her husband had reminded her that it was not her place to judge the righteousness of someone's heart, so she had relented.

Thinking about Andy nearly shattered her self-control. They had both agreed it was best for him not to come on this trip and she was thankful that he was safe at home.

Tears welled up and could not be contained, seeping from her eyes to soak the fabric of the blindfold. Would she make it back home? Would she ever see Andy again? Her heart nearly broke at the thought that she might not.

He would be devastated when he found out she had been taken. They had been married for twenty-one years, together for twenty-four, and were the very definition of soulmates. Neither of them knew how to go through life without the other. He was her world, she was his, and any other romantic clichés you cared to slap on their relationship. Was their marriage perfect, like some kind of fairy tale? Of course not. Squabbles were part of being together and anyone who said otherwise was spitting lies. But they rarely went to bed angry with each other and never let petty disagreements come between them for very long.

She kept Andy in her thoughts as the SUV devoured the miles, drawing strength from their love, their bond. She wasn't sure how long they barreled down the rough road, but it seemed like forever.

The vehicle finally slowed, and she felt it make a right-hand turn. It rolled to a stop, then she heard the driver's window lower with an electric whir. Someone outside the SUV said something in Spanish, the driver responded, and they both laughed throatily. Amber heard the window go back up as the SUV rolled forward once again.

They were not in motion long. The vehicle soon came to a stop and the engine switched off. Doors opened and rough hands hauled her out of the seat and forced her to her knees. She heard the grunts and groans as the other missionaries received the same harsh treatment. Claudia even cried out in pain for a moment but then stopped, the sound of flesh striking flesh making it clear someone had backhanded her into silence. A snarled curse in Spanish punctuated the slap. *"Silencio, puta!"*

Amber quaked inside but steeled herself for whatever came next. She was not naive, not some innocent flower floating through life believing the world was nothing but sunshine and roses. She knew quite well that she might suffer horrible things at the hands of these violent men, the kinds of nightmarish atrocities and violations from which she might never fully recover, even if she somehow managed to survive them.

Someone ripped off her blindfold. She blinked several times, trying to get her eyes to focus. Once they did, she looked around, taking in her surroundings.

She and the other five missionaries were all kneeling in a row next to the SUVs, facing a large barn that had been designed and constructed with a modern retro look. Given that it was late at night, she couldn't see that far into the distance, but they appeared to be on some sort of compound that doubled as a farm. A hacienda-style mansion loomed nearby, lights glowing in the window, the architecture managing to be sleek and current while retaining an old-world feel. Amber saw a shadow move behind a gauzy curtain in one of the upper windows, signifying the house was occupied.

The night air smelled of dung and death.

The stench of shit came from a pigsty attached to the barn, a wood-and-wire fencing system forming a pen from which the hogs could be heard grunting. Through narrow gaps in the wood, Amber glimpsed their large, bloated bodies shuffling through the mud looking for food.

The reek of death came from the half-rotten corpse

hanging on a rough-hewn, bloodstained cross next to the barn.

The poor victim had clearly been human once, but was now nothing more than a decaying, skeletal horror displayed like some kind of macabre artwork. Rags of flesh drooped glutinously from white bones, fluttering like banners in the nocturnal desert breeze. Hollowed eye sockets, plucked clean by birds, stared into whatever abyss awaited after death while the face remained frozen in a rictus of agony. The only thing holding the desiccated remains to the cross were the massive nails driven through the wrists and ankles.

Amber saw the gruesome damage done to the corpse, but it didn't fully register.

She was too busy staring at the clerical collar that hung like a noose around the dead man's neck.

My God, they crucified a priest!

Fresh terror flooded her system, churning her guts and making her blood run cold. An icy ball coalesced in the pit of her stomach as all semblance of hope, the desperate belief that they would somehow survive this, fled like a lamb being chased by a wolf. She struggled to hold on to it, but the putrescent body on the cross clawed at her thoughts like a harbinger of damnation.

She turned her head and glanced over at her companions. Bill and Claudia, ruptured eardrums still leaking blood, stared at the crucifixion scene with their mouths literally hanging open in shock and disgust. Dianne wept and trembled as if the temperature had suddenly dropped to subzero. Gary kept his head bowed, staring fixedly at the ground, refusing to look at the grisly tableau as if bearing witness would leave his soul forever stained. Jack looked on in disbelief, squinting his eyes as if trying to convince himself the corpse was movie magic, not reality.

Amber's heart ached for all of them. How could it not?

I'm so sorry I got you all into this. Please forgive me.

Deep down, she knew she wasn't to blame, but the guilt gnawed at her anyway. This mission trip had been her idea and now they were kneeling in the dirt in front of a crucified priest, hands bound behind their back, under the threat of heavily armed men who had executed another priest right before their eyes just a short time ago.

The journey of faith is as much about suffering as it is about salvation, she had once heard Andy preach. *The Christian walk often has more thorns than roses.* She suspected they were about to find that out the hard way.

A man emerged from the house, bracketed by two armed guards, and approached the missionaries. His steps were steady but unhurried, a man secure in his power, fully aware that everyone would wait on him.

As he drew closer, Amber saw that he was tall for a Mexican, easily pushing six feet, if not an inch or two over. His clean shaven head gleamed under the flood-lamps that illuminated the compound. Gold crucifix earrings pierced his lobes, but they were swiveled upside down. Tattoos ran up his heavily muscled arms, disappearing beneath his shirt, and clawing their way back out up the sides of his neck. As he stopped directly in front of the hostages, Amber noticed that the tattoos were tendrils of flame wrapped around horned skulls. The man breathed heavily, like an angry bull, as if carrying all the extra height and muscle was both burdensome and irritating.

"I am Amando Ochoa," he announced, his voice little more than a guttural growl as his dark eyes boldly raked his captives. "Some people call me *El Crucificador*." He gestured at the cross by the barn. "When it comes to nicknames, I think they really nailed it."

Amber suspected it was an old joke and the chuckles from the guards seemed right on cue, as if had been rehearsed many times before.

"This is my compound," Ochoa continued. "You are my guests here."

"You mean hostages," Jack Spurgeon said with surprising ferocity.

Ochoa's frank, merciless eyes flicked to the young missionary and a cold, cruel smile tugged at the corners of his mustached mouth. "Have I given you a reason to believe that you may speak to me in such a manner?" he asked. "Do I look like someone you should fuck with? Or perhaps you think your God will protect you from my wrath. Is that it?"

"You can't do anything to me unless God lets you."

"Jack!" Amber said. "Be quiet!"

Ochoa ignored her outburst and kept his malevolent gaze focused on Spurgeon. "Then I guess your God wants you to die tonight."

"If God wants my life," Jack replied. "He can have it."

"Rest assured, you Christian *perro*, your life will be taken tonight. But it will not be God that does the taking."

Ochoa turned and gave an order in Spanish to his two bodyguards, who immediately walked over to the cross and got to work taking down the body. How they did it without gagging, Amber had no clue. Watching rotten chunks of meat fall off the bones as the corpse was jostled was enough to make her want to vomit. She swallowed hard to keep the bile down.

Once the remains of the priest were removed from the cross, the two guards heaved the body over the fence into the pigsty. Through the gaps in the wood, Amber saw the herd of hogs hustle over and start devouring the corpse, porcine teeth tearing through putrescent flesh, burrowing into blackened entrails, and cracking open dead bones.

Ochoa saw her staring in horror and chuckled. "The best way to dispose of a dead body," he said. "And the only fitting end for a priest—getting turned into pig shit."

Amber averted her gaze from the pigsty as two hogs started fighting over a coil of intestine like they were playing tug o' war. She considered herself a strong woman but that was more than she needed to see. She looked up at Ochoa. "Why?" she asked softly. "Why are you doing this?"

Ochoa's eyes narrowed, and he seemed to study her more intently. She didn't care for the way his eyes roamed and probed her body as if evaluating all it had to offer, but there was absolutely nothing she could do about it. Whatever he was looking for, Ochoa seemed to find it, then nodded as if satisfied. "You are the leader?" He phrased it as a question, but it was really more of a statement.

Amber nodded. "I am the head of this mission group, yes."

"That is very unfortunate." Ochoa shook his head in mock sadness. "I am afraid you have led this man—" He pointed at Spurgeon. "to his martyrdom."

"No, please."

"*Si*, it is so. Not only will he die *for* Christ, but he will also die *like* Christ."

The two bodyguards lifted the cross out of the hole in the ground and let it drop into the dirt. A cloud of dust roiled up from the impact to momentarily veil the lights.

Ochoa clasped his hands behind his back and began to march back and forth in front of the kneeling mission-aries like a general giving a speech to his frontline troops before battle. He spoke as he walked, boots crunching on the dirt and stones while acid dripped from his words.

"As I was saying before this soon-to-be-dead *cabron* opened his Jesus-loving mouth and interrupted me, you are guests here at my compound, my farm." He shrugged, his shoulders rising and settling in a way that made his powerful muscles ripple. "If you prefer the word 'hostages,' so be it. Because in truth, that is exactly what you are. You are not free to leave and any attempt to escape will be met with severe penalty. You will remain locked in the barn while my ransom demand is sent to your church. If the church pays within the allotted time, your worthless asses will be released."

"Without harm?" Gary Gunther asked.

Ochoa didn't bother responding and his silence said it all.

We're going to suffer, Amber thought, but kept it to herself. The others didn't need to hear it and besides, they already knew. The growing desperation coming off them was as palpable as the dust swirling in the air from the now-prone cross.

"You said we will be released," Amber interjected. "Why should we believe you?"

Ochoa stopped marching, spun on his boot heels, then fixed his eyes on her again. "You should believe me because you have no choice, *puta.*"

"There's always a choice. Even someone like you understands that."

Ochoa smiled, but it was a shark's grin, void of mirth. "Your only choices are to believe you will be set free if my demands are met or believe you will die out here in the desert. The first choice at least offers you some semblance of hope, no? The second choice brings only *desesperación.* Choose hope."

"Please," Amber said. "Please, I'm begging you, can you at least tell me why you're doing this to us?"

"You are paying for the sins of the church. That is all you need to know."

"What did St. Luke's ever do to you?"

Ochoa shook his head. "Not your church specifically. The church as a collective whole. It is corrupt, decayed, perverted beyond all description, and I will continue to punish it for its sins until my dying breath."

"But we're innocent. We didn't do anything to you!"

"You are a Christian, are you not?"

"Yes." She said it proudly, almost defiantly.

"A member of the so-called body of Christ, yes?"

Amber nodded.

"And the body of Christ is called the church, yes?"

"Yes, but—"

"That is good enough for me," Ochoa growled, cutting her off. "The church must be punished for its sins, which means its members must be punished. There is a price to pay for iniquity. Some people pay that price in money, some people pay that price in blood." He pointed at Spurgeon. "Bring him."

"No!" Amber screamed as three guards jerked the young missionary off his knees and dragged him toward the cross.

Spurgeon didn't go easy. He kicked and writhed and hollered, "Let go of me, you bastards!" It was the first time Amber had ever heard him swear and the panic in his voice stabbed at her heart.

He fought valiantly but was no match against the strength of three men. They cut off his flex cuffs before they dropped him onto the cross. He tried to scramble away, but they pinned him down, arms outstretched, one man on each, another holding down his legs. He thrashed against his captors, trying desperately to wrench himself free, but it was useless.

Ochoa disappeared into the barn. When he returned,

he was holding a small sledgehammer and three railroad spikes. Amber couldn't tell if the rust coloring that coated the nails was from corrosion or dried blood.

"No..." she gasped. "No, no, no, oh, please, God, no..."

Spurgeon fought some more, teeth clenched, but to no avail. Three against one, he just didn't have a chance. He spat more curses, using words perhaps not fit for a missionary's mouth, but Amber refused to judge him for it. He was staring down one of the most horrific, torturous executions humanity had ever devised. Who knew what any of them might scream if they were in his shoes?

Ochoa loomed over him, casting a large shadow upon the cross and the doomed man upon it. "Why do you curse me?" the man known as The Crucifier mockingly asked. "You are about to die for your faith. Is that not glorious? You will become a martyr. There is no greater honor, I am told."

"I didn't do anything to you!" Spurgeon shouted, eyes wild with desperation.

"But others did," Ochoa replied. "Others just like you. It is for their *pecados*, for their sins, that you pay."

He kneeled down, pressed the tip of one of the spikes against Spurgeon's left wrist, and raised the hammer.

Please, God, stop this! Amber prayed.

God didn't.

The hammer crashed down against the head of the spike so hard that sparks shot out, the sharp sound of steel striking steel ringing out like a demon's call. The heavy nail ruptured the flesh as it drove between the carpal bones and buried itself in the wood. Blood spurted into the air as Spurgeon's cry of pain split the night, echoing off the barn and sending the hogs into some kind of frenzy. Two more powerful blows from the sledgehammer pounded the head of the spike flush with the missionary's wrist, impaling it to the cross. His fingers curled and spasmed as tortured nerves sent signals of agony to his brain.

Ochoa, moving with the efficiency of someone who had done this many times before, quickly repeated the process on the other wrist and finished up by driving a nail through Spurgeon's overlapped feet. The missionary's cries had broken down into anguished sobs that racked Amber's heart and poured fresh fuel on the flames of her guilt.

Ochoa rose to his full height and made a lifting gesture with the hammer, which was now spackled with red. "Get him up."

The three guards who had held Spurgeon down for his crucifixion now raised the cross, straining and grunting against the weight, and dropped it back into the hole in the ground. The jarring impact wrenched a horrible scream from the missionary's lips.

Ochoa raked his gaze over the remaining five missionaries, letting them all see the hatred and malevolence in his dark eyes, before focusing once again on Amber. "Now you understand why I am called *El Crucificador*."

"What I understand is that you'll burn in hell for this," Amber snapped.

Ochoa shrugged. "Perhaps. Or perhaps there is no hell. Perhaps there is not even a God. I have nailed dozens of God-lovers to that cross over the years and have heard hundreds, maybe even thousands, of prayers hurled to Heaven for God to save them. And yet never once has He bothered to make an appearance." Another shrug. "Even if your beloved God does exist, it would seem He does not care whether His followers live or die by my hands."

"You can shrug it off all you want," Amber said, "but your judgment day is coming."

"You may be right," Ochoa replied. "But your judgment day has already arrived." He held out his hand and one of his men stepped forward to hand him a cell phone that Amber recognized. "This is the *teléfono móvil* that was taken from you. It is yours, *si?*"

Amber saw no point in denying it, so she nodded.

"The passcode, *por favor.*"

She hesitated.

"Give it to me," Ochoa said, "or I will crucify another one."

Amber gave it to him.

"*Gracias.*" Ochoa unlocked the phone, activated the camera function, and began recording a video of Jack Spurgeon hanging on the cross. He even kicked the missionary's nailed feet, eliciting a shriek of pain that he captured in high-definition closeup.

"Stop!" Amber shouted. "Please!"

Ochoa stomped over, drew back his free hand, and slapped her across the face so hard that she thought her jaw might be dislocated. "I will stop when I want to stop, *puta*. We are clear on that, *si?*"

"Please," Amber said, trying to ignore the stinging pain blazing through her cheek. "I'm begging you."

"You will beg, *si*, make no mistake about that," Ochoa replied. "When the time is right, you will beg for mercy." He bent over and leaned in close enough that she could smell his breath, foul and spicy, like rotten meat seasoned with hot chilis. "And there will be none." He stood back up and looked at her phone, using his thumb to scroll. "The priest at your church is Andrew Lillegard, *si?*"

"Yes."

"And he is your husband, *si?*"

How on earth does he know all this? But she didn't ask,

fearful that voicing her question might spark his rage and result in another crucifixion or a severed tongue. She simply nodded.

Ochoa grinned. "I see the question in your eyes. You are wondering how I know so *much, si?* "

"The thought crossed my mind."

Ochoa's grin widened. "I have people everywhere, *señorita*. Even in Sacred Impact Ministries, the organization that brought you here. Despite the scriptures warning them that the love of *dinero* is the root of all evil, so many Christians covet wealth and, just like Judas, will sell out their brothers and sisters for a bagful of silver."

Amber didn't respond but the truth cut deep. She knew it was true because it *had* to be true. What other logical explanation was there? Ochoa knew too much. He clearly had money—with this many armed guards, she suspected he was attached to the Juarez cartel in some way, and far too many followers of Jesus could be swayed when enough greenbacks were waved in front of their faces. Unless evidence to the contrary presented itself, she would go to her grave—sooner rather than later, from the looks of things—believing someone at Sacred Impact Ministries had sold them to slaughter.

She looked at poor Jack Spurgeon nailed to the cross, still writhing in agony, and hoped whoever the traitor was, they burned in hell. Then she immediately felt guilty for her visceral, rather than sacred, response. Christ had prayed for His executioners to be forgiven. As a follower of Christ, she should be doing the same.

But right now, it was so damn hard. *Burn in hell* came a lot easier than *Father, forgive them.*

Ochoa stopped scrolling, turned the phone around, and shoved it in front of her face. It was her contacts list, with all of Andy's information. Except she didn't have him entered as "Andy." The contact name simply said "Hubby."

"Is that your *hombre*?" Ochoa asked. "Your husband?"

Amber saw no point in lying, so she just nodded.

"Excelente." Ochoa put the phone in his pocket and gestured to his men. "Secure the God-lovers in the barn. If any of them give you trouble, cut out their tongues. If they give you more trouble after that, gouge out their eyes. If any of them try to escape, sever all their Achilles tendons."

"What about the women?" one of the guards asked, his eyes bright with lust. "Can we have the *putas*?"

Amber blanched. Further down the line, Claudia and Dianne gasped in terror at the thought of what might be done to them.

Ochoa's eyes danced across each woman's face, a bemused smirk tugging at his lips. "Leave them alone for now," he said, and Amber saw guard's disappointed look. Then Ochoa's smirk wilted, then he stared hard at Amber as he added, "We'll have *mucho* time to play with them later."

Amber swallowed hard and thought, *Dear God in Heaven, where are You?*

FIVE

BACK INSIDE HIS luxuriously appointed house, Armando Ochoa sprawled on a giant, custom-made, four-poster bed that was damn near big enough to dock a battleship. The posts were fashioned from ebony with hand-carved engravings that matched the flaming skull tattoos that adorned his arms. Satin, crimson-hued sheets fitted the mattress, which was soft without being mushy, just the right firmness level to comfortably cradle his heavy, muscular frame.

He propped a pair of large plush pillows behind him for support as he scrolled through Amber Lillegard's cell phone. His plan, finetuned through countless abductions, required him to record a message and send it off, but that could wait for a bit.

Right now, he wanted to get to know the spirited Christian woman locked in his barn.

Amber Lillegard intrigued him. Not just physically, though she was certainly pretty enough for him to consider bedding, and he just might do that before this was over. But beyond her surface appeal, she possessed the kind of fiery steel that he rarely encountered when he captured do-gooder missionaries and dragged them out here to his desert compound. So many of them begged and pleaded and even offered to abandon their beloved God if only Ochoa would spare their miserable lives. Their willingness to sacrifice for their faith seemed to end where the pain and suffering began.

But not this Lillegard *puta*.

Oh, she was clearly scared, all right. How could she not be, given all she had seen and suffered tonight? But behind her frightened eyes burned a fierceness that appealed to him. Not in a merciful way—she was a Christian, after all, and he despised each and every one of them—but the way a warrior appreciates breaking the will of an enemy who refuses to back down, refuses to roll over and bare belly for the fatal blow, refuses to acquiesce without a fight.

Torturing the weak and pitiful was usually enough to slake his thirst for vengeance over the abuse he had endured all those years ago, but crushing a strong spirit made the vengeance that much sweeter.

Amber Lillegard would be broken and Armando 'El Crucificador' Ochoa would savor the breaking.

The nickname had been slapped on him for obvious reasons. Ever since he had nailed his first missionary to the cross and fed the rotten remains to his pigs, the other members of the Juarez cartel in his circle had shaken their heads at his madness and dubbed him The Crucifier. But as long as he kept helping them make money—and letting them use his pigs to dispose of the bodies of their enemies—they tolerated his sadistic, anti-religious fetish. It helped that he funneled a generous portion of the ransom money he collected back into the cartel's coffers.

Ochoa was a mid-level man in the Juarez cartel, and

he not only knew his place, but relished his relative insignificance. He was content with his station. They required nothing more from him than to store drugs in his barns and dump dead bodies in his pigsty. He was richly rewarded for his place in the scheme of things and craved nothing more. Far too often, when it came to ambition in the cartel, you ended up dumped in the desert with a couple of bullets in your brainpan or dangling from a highway overpass with a barbed wire noose around your neck and your belly slit open so your guts could hang out like party streamers.

Keeping your head down and just doing your job was the key to surviving the ruthlessness of cartel affiliation. He had learned this truth early and lived it always.

But if living the cartel life was easy, living with his past was not.

He had only been five years old when the Christian missionaries from a fundamentalist church came to his impoverished, downtrodden village. Ochoa lived with his father, and two brothers, his mother had died from cervical cancer when he was just a baby. He had been so young that he didn't retain a single memory of her and only knew her from the faded photograph his father kept in a cracked plastic frame on the kitchen table. Ochoa knew her face by heart, but she might as well have been a stranger. He sometimes wondered if he would have turned out differently had he known a mother's love and maternal nurturing.

The missionaries brought food and medical supplies, all of which were gratefully welcomed by the villagers. But they also carried a troubling message that Catholics—of which the village primarily consisted of—were not really Christians and would therefore burn in Hell when they died. They urged the villagers to renounce their traditional Catholicism and turn to the Protestant way of faith.

For the most part, the turn-or-burn message had fallen on deaf ears—the Catholic faith was deeply entrenched in Mexico, with well over three-quarters of the country claiming it as their religious affiliation—but Ochoa's father had been one of the few who converted.

In the wake of this conversion, the missionaries convinced his father that Ochoa and his brothers would be better off at the Messiah of Mercy Home for Children, a Christian school/orphanage not far from Chihuahua City. Allegedly, they would receive better food, better healthcare, better education, and be raised in the Christian faith to better prepare them for eternal life in Heaven.

But instead of Heaven, the school introduced them to hell.

The brothers barely had time to acclimate to their new home before the abuse started. The brutality knew no limits, the headmaster of the school a rigid believer that pain and torture exorcised the demons from children's souls. The punishments, for infractions both real and imagined, started with being forced to eat rancid, maggot-infested food, and only escalated from there.

They were chained in the cellar for days at a time, in total blackness. They were beaten, first with rods, then with a crudely fashioned cat-o'-nine-tails scourge the headmaster carried with him at all times. Their bodies became crisscrossed with scars as the headmaster and the other staff working at the Messiah of Mercy Home for Children showed them exactly what their version of the love of Jesus looked like.

The sexual abuse started a little later. Ochoa was spared at first—apparently not even the twisted, ghoulish perverts running the school were into boys that young—

but his brothers, only a few years older, were often violated in whatever sick ways the "Christians" needed in order to satisfy their unholy appetites. Ochoa was often forced to watch, knowing he was looking at his own future.

It took nearly three years, but the horrors they were forced to endure eventually killed his brothers. One of them resisted the "affections" of one of the teachers and was beaten so badly that he died from his wounds that night. Two days later, the other brother committed suicide. Ochoa found him dead on the cold tile floor of a bathroom, arms opened from wrists to elbows. He remembered being shocked by how much blood the human body could hold.

The day after they buried both of them in a single, shallow grave, Ochoa was raped for the first time.

The headmaster summoned him to his office under the guise of "comforting him in his time of grief." But after reading a few trite scripture verses and uttering hollow platitudes about his brothers being in a better place, the man's evil rose to the forefront and eight-year-old Ochoa found himself stripped bare and his buttocks scourged raw before being forcefully violated. Even to this day, the searing pain and bestial grunts of the headmaster haunted his nightmares.

Barely old enough to fully comprehend what had happened—what had been done—to him, Ochoa nevertheless vowed vengeance on the man who had hurt him and robbed him of his brothers.

It took four years—four years of unimaginable suffering—but one day after another "session" in the headmaster's office, Ochoa took the knife he had stolen from the kitchen and secreted under his shirt and stabbed his tormentor in the throat, severing the vocal cords and ensuring the man could not cry out for help. As the sick, sanctimonious *bastardo* gurgled and died, Ochoa stabbed him seventy-seven more times, until his face, neck, chest, and belly were nothing but a ragged red ruin. For his coup de grace, he chopped the *cabron's* cock off and crammed it down his blood-choked throat.

Then he set the orphanage on fire and danced in front of the flames as it burned to the ground.

But like a thirsty man given only a few drops of water, his vengeance was not yet satisfied. The murdered head-master might have done most of the actual torturing, but it was the missionaries who had lured him from his village with false promises and served him up as a sacrificial lamb to dark, demented lusts.

More people needed to pay. His need for revenge had not been slaked.

He had walked away from the ashes of the orphanage and eked out a living on the streets before finding his way into the cartel lifestyle. He spent his teenage years as a low-level peon doing the gutter-level dirty work, but by the time he reached his early twenties, he was starting to make a name for himself and continued his upward trajectory until he found himself here, on a hacienda in the Chihuahuan desert.

With his place in the cartel empire established, Ochoa turned his attention back to the hunger for vengeance that had festered in him for the last decade, like a simmering pot on a back burner left to bubble and curdle into something dark and poisonous. It now boiled over and he set about putting his plans for revenge into motion.

Paying off people in the various missionary organizations had proven to be far easier than expected, and he received frequent updates on churches undertaking mission trips in his territory. He began abducting the groups, crucifying one to make an example and indulging his need for bloody vengeance, and then ransoming the rest. He was always careful to only kill one and free the others once the money was received; if he became known as a man who slaughtered everyone after ransoms were paid, then soon nobody would pay the ransom. That would be problematic, for the cartel only tolerated his "hobby" because of the ransom money he funneled into their coffers.

Ochoa stared up at the ceiling and wondered if it would ever be enough. Not the money. The killing. Could he ever slay enough missionaries to feel avenged for what had happened to him? Could he ever shed enough Christian blood to feel satisfied that the debt for his suffering and shame had been fully paid?

Questions without answers. But this much he knew—the day of "enough" had not come yet. So he would continue to do what he had done for so many years now.

He held Amber's phone up in front of his face, activated the video function, and began recording. As always, he kept it fairly simple and to the point.

"Andy—or should I call you *Padre*?—you do not know who I am, but I have your wife, as well as the other missionaries you were foolish enough to send to my country. For the sins of the church, both past, present, and future, one of them has already been sent to Hell—you will witness his death at the end of this message—and the rest will be executed in three days if you do not comply with my demand, which is very simple: pay me $500,000 and your wife and the others will be released. Fail to pay, and they will all taste the nails. Also, I will bring your wife to my bed and make her beg for death by the time I am through with her. Information on where to wire the money will be sent in a separate message. Again, you have three days to comply. They may have faith in God, but it is you who truly controls their fate."

He ended the recording, watched it from start to finish to check for any glitches, and then spliced the crucifixion video onto the beginning before hitting "Send."

Father Andy Lillegard was about to have a very bad day.

SIX

ANDY AWAKENED SHORTLY after dawn as the first rays of the sun brightened the window shades of his bedroom. He kept meaning to buy blackout blinds but never got around to it. The old air conditioner in the window rumbled away, loud but reliable, and the temperature in the room was cool and comfortable, a barrier against the sticky humidity he had been dealing with when he hit the sheets last night. People thought the northern Adirondacks were always cold, but in reality, the summers could get blazing hot in July and August. Still, it was better than the brutal, six-month winters the region endured every year. Thankfully, his time in Wisconsin had prepared him for those.

He yawned, stretched, rubbed the sleep from his eyes, and let his hand fall onto the empty space in the bed next to him. Normally, Amber would be curled up there, bundled under an extra blanket or two to combat the cold of the air conditioner. He felt an ache of loneliness as he missed his wife, but a warm smile also softened his face as he thought of her with pride—the good kind, not the bad kind. He was really proud of her for leading that mission trip, thankful to have a spouse who loved the Lord and complimented his ministry with faith work of her own.

The smile switched to a frown as he remembered that he had not heard from her last night before drifting off to sleep. Not a big deal; before she left, they had discussed the fact that she would be busy and that her check-ins might be sporadic. Still, he had expected to hear from her once she reached Holy Spirit Anglican Church and settled into the dormitory there. The people at Sacred Impact Mission Group had assured them there was ample cell service in that area.

He reached for his phone on the nightstand and breathed a sigh of relief when he saw the notification that he had received a text message from her long after he went to bed. The phone wasn't on silent mode but apparently the rumbling drone of the air conditioner had drowned out the notification chime. Or maybe he had just slept through it. Sometimes he slept so deeply that he was afraid he might miss the Rapture if Christ came back at night.

He swiped away the notification, navigated to his texts, saw that Amber had sent a video, and tapped the screen to make it play.

Disbelief was his first reaction as he watched the brutal crucifixion of Jack Spurgeon. The horror didn't really hit until the camera panned away from the screaming man on the cross and scanned across the missionaries kneeling in the dirt with their hands bound behind their backs and he saw his wife. The sight of Amber in that state caused panic to seize his heart and the blood freeze in his veins.

"No, no, no, no, no…" he whispered like a mantra, a desperate, chanting prayer. This wasn't happening. He must still be asleep, trapped in a nightmare. He just needed to wake up. His brain shouted at him, demanding and insistent. *Wake up, Andy! Wake up!*

Then he listened to the man's ransom demands and threats to torture and crucify Amber and realized this was all too real. The shock and terror and grief punched him deep in the guts like a cold, hard, heavy fist. He set the phone down as if it might burn him if he held it any longer, swung his legs out of bed, rested his elbows on his knees, buried his face in his hands, and broke down in anguished sobs that racked his trembling frame from scalp to soles.

No, no, no, no, this can't be happening.

How long he stayed like that, he wasn't certain. Two minutes? Two hours? Time ceased to exist. But eventually, somehow, he managed to claw his way back up through the horror and when he surfaced into reality again, time lurched back into gear. At that moment, his inarticulate cries became fervent prayers. Not just because he was a priest and that's what priests were supposed to do. No, it was more than that. So much more than that.

He prayed because he truly believed that when the world was falling part, when all hope seemed lost, God was the one you should turn to. Despite the heart-wrenching, savage, unexpected blow he had just taken, he knew God was in control, and so that's where he turned for strength and comfort. Not for himself—for Amber.

The prayers he prayed were raw, unpretty, lacking even the faintest whiff of ritualistic polish. He didn't grab the Bible or turn to the Book of Common Prayer for the "right" words. He simply poured out his soul, poured out his fears, and cried out for answers that he fully knew might never come. *Why is this happening?* is a question that God rarely chose to answer, leading priests, pastors, and preachers to resort to trite platitudes such as *the Lord works in mysterious ways* or *His ways are not our ways.* Andy knew this because he far too often resorted to them himself. Distressed parishioners craved some kind of response, no matter how hollow, rather than the silence of uncertainty.

When he was done praying for answers he doubted he would ever receive, crying out against the injustice of it all, pleading with God to be with Amber, and pouring out his rage and anguish with words both ugly and heartfelt, he finally wiped the tears from his face and took a deep, shaky breath. As he exhaled, long and slow, he managed to wrangle his emotions back under control and his next prayer was calmer, more deliberate and pointed.

"Dear God, please bring my wife back to me. I don't have the money, I don't have the means, I have no idea how to accomplish this. Her only hope is You, so I'm asking You for a miracle. Tell me what I should do. In Christ's name..."

The *Amen* had no sooner left his lips than a single thought filled his mind.

Call Stone.

SEVEN

STONE PULLED on a light flannel shirt before he headed out to the barn, Max ambling along behind him with a woe-is-me look that seemed to say, *It's too early for this crap, man.* It was the same look the Shottie wore on his scarred-up face any morning he came out with Stone. The dog wasn't much of an early riser, sometimes choosing to stay inside and catch some extra winks while Stone went out and took care of Rocky, his Appaloosa stallion. But this morning Max had yawned, stretched so hard that you could almost hear the muscles popping, and opted to tag along, his only complaint the grumbly look he wore.

It was supposed to climb into the upper seventies later today, but at the crack of dawn, the air still held some coolness, the sun cresting over the nearby mountains promising heat that it had not yet delivered. It might be July, but this was the northern Adirondacks, and Stone could faintly see his breath as he slid open the barn door and was greeted with a friendly nicker from Rocky. Unlike Max, Rock was rarely, if ever, grumpy.

Stone had rescued the horse from abusive owners last year and the Appaloosa seemed eternally grateful.

"Morning to you, too, you old nag." Stone ruffled the stallion's forelock, the tuft of hair that fell between a horse's ears down toward the eyes and debated whether or not he had time to saddle up for a quick ride before heading to work. It had been too long since he'd given the horse a good workout.

He scooped some oats into the feed bucket and Rocky started munching away contentedly. Stone picked up a metal comb off the shelf and started working out the tangles in the stallion's mane. Sometimes it reminded him of brushing his daughter Jasmine's hair before she died and made tears well up in his eyes as the painful sting of loss took its toll. Sometimes those tears would even escape and slide down his cheeks, leaving behind silvery tracks of grief and pain, before dripping onto the straw-covered floor of the stable.

In those moments, the often-aloof Max would lift his big head from the pile of clean straw he rested on in the corner and give him a look that managed to be both sad and supportive. Like most dogs, the Shottie seemed tuned in to his master's emotions. Stone would have hidden his tears from most people but in front of Max, he openly wept sometimes.

But not this morning. This morning, he whistled while he worked. And in between the whistling, he talked to Max about whatever was on his mind, mostly the sins of his past. It was something he did more and more frequently these days, almost like a confessor spilling his guts to a priest. Except in this case, the priest had four legs and had no idea how to grant absolution.

Best kind of priest, Stone thought. *A big, loveable mutt that can't talk.*

Stone told him about his warrior days, the years in

black ops, the years spent killing for the government, the notches on his gun, the corpses on his conscience. He told him about the death of his daughter, the failure of his marriage, and his walking away from the world of government-sanctioned wet work. He told him about finding God, seeking some sort of redemption for the bloodshed of his past, and how he became a preacher.

He even told the dog about his failure—maybe even inability—to leave the violence behind. He pontificated about the sense of primal justice that consumed him like a smoldering fire that sometimes erupted into an inferno that burned away doubts and reluctance and hesitation. He told him about the guilt that sometimes showed up in the aftermath of his vigilante ways and then admitted that the guilt was lessening with every bullet fired, every blade bloodied, every evildoer put six feet under.

"Not sure what all of that says about me, Max," Stone murmured quietly as he set the comb back down on the shelf and patted Rocky on the neck. "But whatever it is, I'm learning to live with it. Maybe I'll need forgiveness for it someday, but if that's the case, I know God'll be there to give it."

Max sighed and shot him a look that seemed to say, *Are you done rambling? Can we go back inside now? It's time for breakfast.*

Stuck in the back pocket of his jeans, Stone's phone chimed and vibrated. He pulled it out and saw that it was Andy calling. His face furrowed into a frown. Something told him this wasn't good news. Andy never called him this early.

He answered, putting the phone on speaker. "Morning, Andy."

Without preamble, Andy blurted, "Luke, they've taken her."

"What're you talking about? Taken who?"

"Amber!" Andy's voice sounded panicked, brittle, a man on the edge who was barely holding on. "Her and the other missionaries have been kidnapped. They already killed Jack Spurgeon. They crucified him, Luke. *Crucified him*, for god's sake! They're demanding a half-million dollars or they'll kill the rest of them."

Stone clenched his jaw as something dark, cold, and dangerous uncoiled deep down inside him.

Andy stammered, "I...I didn't know who else...who else to call. I was praying and...and I just felt led to reach out to you for help."

"You're damn right I'll help," Stone said. "I'll be there in thirty minutes."

What he left unspoken was that when he said *help*, what he really meant was *kill them all*.

———

A half hour later, Stone's opinion of what he would do to the kidnappers had not changed. Right or wrong, mercy wasn't on the agenda. The bastards could ask God for mercy after Stone punched their one-way ticket to the other side of the grave.

He sat in Andy's living room and watched the video, gritting his teeth in fury as he witnessed the crucifixion of Jack Spurgeon, the half-million-dollar ransom demand, and the threat to violate Amber. He stared at the kidnapper's face, memorizing the angry features, the cold eyes, the sneering lips, as he silently vowed to terminate the son of a bitch for the atrocities he had committed. Maybe he would take the nails from the cross and hammer them through the fucker's face.

Andy slumped on the couch and rubbed his stubbled face with trembling hands. The Episcopalian priest looked like he had aged twenty years since Stone had visited him yesterday, his features haggard and carved up by stress fissures. Certainly understandable, given what the man was going through right now.

"I don't have that kind of money, Luke," Andy said. "And as you know, we're a small congregation, and none of our members are particularly wealthy. Certainly not wealthy enough to just hand over five hundred thousand dollars."

"I doubt it would do much good anyway," Stone replied. "More likely than not, this asshole would just take your money, put a bullet in the back of everyone's heads, and dump their bodies out in the desert somewhere."

Andy blanched. "I was afraid you were going to say that." He gnawed at his lower lip, then asked, "So what do we do?"

"Go down there, find this piece of shit, put a few dozen bullets in him, and bring your people home."

Andy looked stricken. "You know I can't do that, Luke."

"Can't?" Stone leveled a direct stare at him. "Or won't?"

"You know God has called me to a life of nonviolence."

"You don't think maybe God might make an exception in this case?"

Andy looked pained as he replied, "I think God expects us to keep our vows to Him, no matter the cost, no matter the sacrifice."

"Even if it means Amber gets raped and killed?"

Andy swallowed hard but said nothing.

Stone didn't press the issue. Instead, he asked, "So what's your plan to get her back?"

Andy cleared his throat, looked him straight in the eye, and said, "Ask you to do it."

Stone met his gaze. "Not gonna lie, Andy, I'm not sure how I feel about someone asking me to get my hands dirty so theirs can stay clean."

Andy leaned forward and spoke earnestly. "Luke, you know me well enough to know that I would like nothing more than to grab some guns, march down there, kick some ass, kill some bastards, and get Amber back."

"There's nothing stopping you."

"*God* is stopping me," Andy replied, his tone edgy and heated. He looked at Stone, long and hard. "And who knows, maybe you were brought into my life for just this very reason."

"Maybe," Stone conceded. The thought had already crossed his mind, because God had a way of bringing you the right people at the right time. "But there's no way of knowing that for sure."

"What I *do* know is that you used to do this kind of work," Andy said. "I may not know all the gory details, nor do I need to, but I know you are—or at least, were—a trigger puller." He shuffled forward until he was sitting on the edge of the sofa. "I'm asking you—no, *begging* you —to rescue Amber and the other missionaries."

"Do you really know what you're asking?" Stone fixed his friend with a piercing stare. "I'll be breaking enough laws that, if I get caught, I'll wind up rotting in a Mexican prison for the rest of my life. I spent some time in a prison once and didn't much care for it. And even if I don't get caught, I'll be stacking bodies left and right." He paused, making sure his next words sank in. "Make no mistake, Andy, if I do this, I'm going to kill the moth-erfuckers that did this so that they can never do it again."

"Vengeance." Andy practically whispered the word, as if saying it too loud might taint their souls.

"Not vengeance," Stone countered. "Justice."

"You really believe there is justice outside the law?"

"Sometimes that's the *only* place there's justice."

Andy waved a hand dismissively. Not toward Stone, but toward the topic. "Listen, Luke, I really don't care about any of that right now. All I care about is getting Amber and the others back and if you're willing to do that for me, I'm not going to question your methods. If I hadn't made a vow to the Lord, I would be doing the exact same thing myself, the law be damned."

Stone didn't respond, different thoughts careening through his mind like ricochets. The warrior side of him resented a man who sat out a battle while others took the risk. Right or wrong, that's just the way he felt. But as a preacher, he fully respected someone who stuck to their guns—figuratively speaking—and proved their devotion to God by not abandoning their vows when the going got tough.

"I'll do it," he finally said. "I've got a contact from my old life that can get me into Mexico on the down low and hopefully provide some intel. I'll give them a call, see if I can get the ball rolling."

"Thank Christ," Andy breathed, and it was not even close to a blasphemy.

Stone continued, "But I want to make it absolutely clear that there's going to be killing and most likely, lots of it. You may not fire the bullets or stick the blade, but by asking me to do the dirty work, there's going to be blood on your conscience, and I need to know you can live with that."

Andy nodded without hesitation. "I understand completely. Believe me, I do. As long as I get my wife back, I'll live with the cost and ask God for forgiveness."

"Good." Stone stood up and settled his Stetson on his head. "Because we're both gonna need it when this is over."

EIGHT

STONE WAS USUALLY CONSIDERATE ENOUGH NOT to call people this early in the morning —not everyone liked to rise 'n shine at the crack of dawn —but with lives at stake and a doomsday clock ticking down toward a fatal deadline, he couldn't afford to waste any time.

Braxx answered on the fourth ring and sounded sleepier than a sloth overdosing on downers. "Do you have any idea what time it is, you fucking nimrod? This damn well better be a matter of life or death."

"Both, actually," Stone replied. "One death so far and five lives that need saving."

"Oh, shit." The sound of fabric rustling and springs creaking, presumably as Braxx sat up in bed. "Sorry for answering the phone like a prick." All the slumber had vanished from his voice like vapor in the hot sun. "Tell me what you got."

"If you didn't answer the phone like a prick, I'd figure I had the wrong number," Stone said.

"You've got a point there," Braxx replied. "I'll give you that."

"All right," Stone said, buckling right down to business. "Here's the sitrep…"

He relayed everything to Braxx in short, succinct sentences, keeping it simple but making sure his buddy got all the pertinent details. No sugarcoating; he wanted Braxx to know exactly what was going down, the lay of the land, what the hell they were getting into.

When he finished, Stone waited for Braxx's response. He heard heavy breathing on the other end of the line that almost sounded dirty, but Stone knew from personal experience that sound was just Braxx's chest heaving in anger. "Those rotten sons of bitches," he growled. "Those rotten, no good, testicle-sucking sons of bitches. Tell me you're gonna burn 'em to the ground and piss on the ashes before flushing 'em all down to hell."

"That's the basic plan, yeah," Stone said. "But I could use your help. Need someone to watch my six."

"Fucking-A, bro. You know I'll ride shotgun for you."

"You're right, I know you will. But I need to know that Monica is okay with it."

"She'll be fine."

"Ask her, Braxx. With the phone on. I want to hear her say it."

"You're a real pain in my ass, Stone."

"This is dangerous shit, brother, and you have a wife who will be putting roses on your grave if this thing goes sideways. She has a right to have a say in this."

"You know what she's going to say. She knows what we used to do. I didn't marry some weak-ass, fragile flower fairy of a woman who clutches her pearls and gasps hysterically at the first hint of danger. I also didn't marry the kind of woman who will ever turn her back on a friend."

"You're right, Braxx. You married a good woman. A *damn* good woman. But I still want you to ask her."

"Like I said, buddy, you're a royal pain in the keister." Braxx heaved a longsuffering sigh as if he bore all the burdens of the world on his shoulders. But Stone heard the sound of him climbing out of bed and shuffling somewhere.

"Are you still wearing those stupid bunny slippers?" he asked.

"You know it, baby," Braxx replied. "Pinker than fresh...well, you're a preacher now, so I won't say it. But yeah, pinker than that and twice as comfortable."

"You've got serious issues, man."

"Maybe," Braxx conceded. "But the pink bunny slippers help me deal with them."

A few moments later, Stone heard the sound of dishes clinking together and something sizzling. "Is she making your lazy ass breakfast?" he asked. "I swear I can hear bacon cooking."

"You know it." Stone could practically hear Braxx grinning through the phone. "Told you she's a good woman."

"The fact that she married you is proof that God smiles on the unjust."

"Hurtful," Braxx said. "This is normally where I'd tell you to go stuff a cactus up your ass sideways but I'm kind of busy right now." He then proceeded to spell everything out for Monica.

Stone listened without saying anything. He would head into Mexico by himself if it came down to that— God knew he'd gone into one-man-army mode before— but the mission would have a higher chance of success with Braxx by his side. But there was no doubt they would be up against difficult odds. Sure, they both excelled at the blood-and-thunder business, but everyone's luck ran out at some point, and it was your turn to dance with the Reaper. Their mission might be righteous that but wouldn't make them bulletproof. If Monica didn't want Braxx to go, didn't want him to put his life on the line for people he didn't know, Stone wouldn't blame her.

But as it turned out, he had nothing to worry about.

"I would never ask you to turn your back on a friend," Monica said once Braxx had finished relaying the situation. "Honey, you know that."

"I do know that," Braxx replied. "And that's exactly what I told him. But you know Luke. He's a stubborn dipshit sometimes."

Stone said, "You know I can hear you, right?"

"I sure as hell hope so," Braxx replied. "No point in wasting a good insult that doesn't reach those hat-holders you call ears."

"If that's your idea of a good insult, you need to up your game."

"Kiss my ass."

"How original."

"Besides," Monica said, ignoring the brothers-in-arms banter, "you wouldn't even be alive if it wasn't for Luke. We'll never forget what he did for you in Syria. If he needs your help, then you're damn well going to help him."

"You hear that?" Braxx asked. "You good now? I'm tagging along to watch your six."

"Yeah, I'm good," Stone replied. "Happy to have you. You know my motto: two guns are always better than one."

"You know where the missionaries are being held?"

"Not yet."

"So what's your plan to get intel once we hit Mexico?"

"I'm going to reach out to Bianca."

Braxx let out a long, low whistle of surprise. "Bianca, huh? Playing with fire there, bro."

"Tell me something I don't know," Stone replied.

"Have you talked to her since the good ol' days?"

"She sent me a card when Jasmine died."

"Well, that's something, I guess." Braxx didn't sound convinced. "You got a plan B in case plan A kicks you in the balls and tells you to get bent?"

"I'll figure something out."

"Living on faith and a prayer, got it." Braxx changed subjects. "Where you want me to meet you?"

"Meet me at the airport in El Paso tonight. I should have more information by then."

"Let's hope so," Braxx said. "Because if you don't, we're up shit creek and not only do we not have a paddle, our boat's got a bunch of fucking holes in it."

———

Having secured Braxx's promise to back him up, Stone headed over to the Birch Bark Diner to see Holly. Even with a timeclock ticking, he couldn't just ride off on a dangerous mission without saying goodbye. They might be "just good friends," but he owed her more than that. Hell, he owed *himself* more than that. A text might have been easier, but he didn't want to head off to war without seeing her again, knowing there was a chance it might be the last time. Because nobody dodged death forever.

She couldn't give him her full attention because of the breakfast rush, which was understandable and disappointing at the same time, but in between orders, she listened as he explained everything to her, keeping his voice low so he wouldn't be overheard by anyone else in the diner.

"I understand why you're going," she said. "Really, I do. But I wish you didn't have to."

"I'm their best shot at getting out of this alive."

"Aren't there people who handle this kind of thing? The CIA or the State Department or something like that? Something that makes more sense than a couple of guys going all Rambo in a foreign country?"

"Sure, there are people, but the bureaucratic red tape would be a nightmare. By the time anything official could be organized, the missionaries would be dead," Stone replied. "The best course of action is a covert, unsanctioned infiltration and rescue."

"And termination, right?" she said softly.

"What?"

"You're going to kill whoever did this, whoever took them, aren't you." It wasn't a question and there was no judgment in her tone. How could there be? She had killed people herself in the name of survival and revenge and she was no hypocrite.

"I'm going to do whatever needs to be done," Stone replied and left it at that. Nothing more needed to be said, because they both knew exactly what he meant.

She stepped close and put a hand on his chest. "Then go do what you have to do and get your ass back here, cowboy."

"You mind taking care of Max and Rocky for a few days?"

"Of course not. Put them right out of your mind. I've got that covered."

"Thanks."

"Promise me you'll come back, Luke."

"I'm not really one for making promises I don't know for sure I can keep."

"Just say it." There was a tremor in Holly's voice. "I need to hear you say the words."

Stone would do anything for her, including making a comforting promise that might end up broken. "I promise I'll come back, Holly."

Her fingers tightened against his chest, bunching in his shirt for just a moment, and then she stepped back and looked up at him with eyes that seemed to be searching for something. Whether she found it or not, she gave no hint. "You damn well better," she said with a small, brave smile, and then pushed him toward the door. "Now get out of here and go save the world."

———

Back in the '78 Chevy Blazer, heading home to pack a bag —just clothes, since he and Braxx would acquire weapons and gear in Mexico—Stone reflected on the strange, uncertain nature of his relationship with Holly. They both had emotional landmines they tap-danced around by a mostly unspoken, mutual agreement, but Stone wasn't convinced the *more-than-friends-but-not-quite-lovers* nature of what existed between them was sustainable for much longer. She deserved a man who would take her in his arms, not one that kept her at arm's length.

As the phrase went, it was time to fish or cut bait. Or stop burning daylight, as the old cowboys used to say.

But now was not the time to ponder the predicament. It was go-time, and any warrior worth his salt knew that thinking about the ones left behind while on a mission was a recipe for disaster. Worrying about everything you had to lose caused your focus to falter and loss of focus in a kill-zone got you dead.

Getting dead wasn't on Stone's agenda, so he pushed thoughts of Holly to the back burner. He would deal with that if and when he got back from dispensing some primal justice. Because Holly had been right—termination was definitely on the menu.

The bastard down in Mexico might like crucifying Christians with extreme prejudice but Stone intended to come down on the son of a bitch like the hammer of God and nail his ass to the fucking wall.

NINE

HOLLY WATCHED BEMUSEDLY as Lizzy inhaled the last strand of spaghetti off her plate with the loudest, least ladylike slurp imaginable, leaving tomato sauce slathered on her lips. Her seventeen-year-old daughter pretended to be a dainty eater when company was around but when it was just her and Holly, good table manners often went out the window.

"That good, huh?" Holly asked, arching an eyebrow.

Lizzy popped the last meatball in her mouth, chewed, swallowed, and nodded. "The best." She wiped the sauce off her lips with a napkin.

"It's just a box of angel hair pasta and a can of dollar store meat sauce with some frozen meatballs thrown in. Not exactly gourmet cuisine. You know I can't cook for crap."

"That's why it's the best. You didn't really cook." Lizzy grinned and winked at her.

"If I had known teenagers grew up to be so sassy, I would have spanked you more as a child."

Lizzy made a *tsk-tsk* sound. "Haven't you heard?

That's a no-no. You can't spank anymore. It's considered child abuse."

"Yeah, well, making fun of your mother's cooking skills—or lack thereof—is considered elderly abuse, so you'd best watch yourself, young lady," Holly replied with a smile. She genuinely enjoyed spending time with her daughter, acutely aware that she wouldn't have her at home that much longer. The thought made her heart hurt.

Lizzy set her silverware on her plate and started to push her chair back. "I need to start studying for this stupid chemistry quiz tomorrow."

"Hold on a second," Holly said. "I need to tell you something."

Lizzy leaned forward, resting her elbows on the table. "Okay, but can you make it quick? Eric is coming over to study and he'll be here soon."

"Did I know about this?"

"I texted you after school and told you."

"Guess I missed it."

"Mom…"

"Relax," Holly teased. "Far be it from me to get in the way of young love."

Lizzy rolled her eyes. Like all teenage girls, she was a master at it and had practically turned it into an artform. "Jeez, Mom, don't make me gag."

"Wait…you're not in love?"

"I'm seventeen, not thirty-seven. We're dating, that's all. Little early to be throwing the L-word around."

"Eric seems like a nice boy."

Another eye roll, this one even better than the last. "Please, Mom, for the love of all that is holy, do not call him a boy when he's here."

"What is he, then?"

"He's a guy."

"Well, is he a *guy* friend or a *boy*friend?"

"You're insufferable sometimes, you know that, right?"

"One of my many endearing qualities."

A third, and totally majestic, eye roll. "What did you want to tell me?"

"It's about Luke."

Lizzy instantly looked worried. She and Stone had shared a bond pretty much from the moment they met, but it had deepened after the death of Lizzy's father last year, despite the fact that it was Stone who had gunned him down. "Is he okay?"

"He's fine," Holly assured her. *For now, anyway.* "But he's going to be out of town for a few days, maybe longer, depending on how things go."

"The only time he's ever left town is to go visit his daughter's grave in Texas," Lizzy said with a frown. "Is that where he's going?"

"He'll be in Texas briefly to meet an old friend, and then they're heading to Mexico."

Lizzy's eyes widened in exaggerated shock. "Luke has friends?"

Holly smiled. "Everyone has friends, Liz."

"That's not true and you know it. Heck, I can rattle off twenty kids at school who have to sit by themselves at lunch."

"Well, you may be right, but Luke does have friends. At least one, anyway. From his…you know, old days."

"Wait." Lizzy's eyes narrowed. "This friend is from back before Stone became a preacher?"

"Yes. They've known each other for a long time, I guess."

Lizzy's eyes narrowed even more, now nothing but suspicious slits. "And what, exactly, are they doing in Mexico? Because somehow I doubt that they're going down there for the margaritas."

Holly fidgeted. It wasn't that Lizzy couldn't be trusted with the truth, the whole truth, and nothing but the truth, but she didn't want to worry her. Her daughter had been through enough hell and heartache in her young life and Holly didn't want her lying awake at night chewing her fingernails down to the raw, bleeding nubs because Stone was off doing dangerous things. *That will be my job.*

She decided the simple truth without the worrisome details would suffice. "They're going down there to help a missionary group."

This elicited yet another eye roll. "You're a terrible liar, mom. I mean, you lie even worse than you cook. I can't believe you used to work in a casino because your poker face is about as bad as it gets."

"I'm telling you the truth."

"Not all of it, that's plain to see."

"I can't tell you all of it, Lizzy. For that matter, *I* don't even know all the details. Luke only told me what he thought I needed to know."

"But it's dangerous, right? That's why you're trying to tell me as little as possible."

Holly sighed and relented. "It might be, yes."

"*Might* be or *will* be?"

"There's a dangerous aspect to it, yes," Holly replied. "The missionaries are in trouble and Luke and his friend are going to try and help them."

The worried look immediately returned to Lizzy's face, which was exactly what Holly had been trying to avoid. "How dangerous? Like, he's going to be okay, right? He's going to come back?"

"Lizzy, relax." Holly reached over and touched her daughter's hand. "We've seen Luke take down a child-trafficking ring, we've seen him bust up a meth-cooking operation, we've seen him survive a neo-Nazi assault on the police station, and he singlehandedly took out your father's entire army last year. If he survived all that—not to mention all the stuff he did before we even knew him —I don't think we need to be too worried about what he's doing in Mexico."

"The cartels are really violent, right? Like, scary violent? What if Luke is tangling with a drug cartel?"

"Then God help the cartels," Holly said.

"God help *us* if he doesn't come back," Lizzy muttered. She looked at her mother, eyes bright and worried. "Mom, I'm not sure what I would do without Luke in my life."

"Neither do I, so let's pray he comes back safe and sound."

Lizzy smiled. "You know, you need to lock that cowboy down. Hogtie him if you have to."

"Why can't we just be friends?"

"You can," Lizzy replied. "But you're not. There's something between you and Luke and don't even try to deny. Heck, a blind man could see it."

"It's complicated," Holly replied. "We've both been hurt in the past and sometimes that makes things hard."

Lizzy sniffed derisively. "Sounds like you two are letting your pasts ruin your present and future."

"You get that from a fortune cookie or something?"

Lizzy grinned. "Nah, some movie I watched on Netflix the other day."

"So glad I'm getting romance advice from a streaming service."

"Speaking of romance," Lizzy said as they both heard the crunch of gravel under tires in the driveway, "sounds like Eric is here for our study date."

A car door slammed and a few moments later, Eric strolled in through the back door that led into the kitchen and dining room. "Hey, Liz," he greeted, followed by a polite nod to Holly. "Evening, Ms. Bennett."

Holly smiled. "Hello, Eric." She had to admit that he was a good-looking young man, with a thick head of light brown hair that he wore in a deliberately messy style. His eyes sparkled with intelligence, his face always seemed to wear a charmingly roguish smile, and he had the lean build of a tennis player rather than the bulldozer brawn of a football jock.

He had been nothing but perfectly polite and respectful during their interactions so far. Holly's last semi-serious boyfriend had been a senior who damn near molested her right here on the living room sofa, so Eric was a welcome and refreshing change. She knew teenage romances often flared hot, burned out, and died fast, but she wouldn't be sorry if this one lasted a little while. And maybe, being a pastor's son, he would be less likely to put his hands where they didn't belong. Then again, boys will be boys, and Holly wasn't naive.

Lizzy took her plate over to the sink and then said, "We're heading upstairs."

Holly smirked at both of them. "To study, right?"

Eric nodded. "You know it, Ms. Bennett. This pre-calc stuff is really kicking our butts."

"Thought you were studying for chemistry," Holly said, giving Lizzy a look and arching her eyebrows.

Lizzy blushed slightly.

Eric tried to swoop in with a half-assed rescue. "Uh, it's both, actually."

Holly smiled. "Well, don't ask me for help with that pre-calc stuff. All I know about math I learned from dealing blackjack, so unless the question is 'What beats twenty?', I don't know the answer."

"That's why I'm studying with him, not you," Lizzy

said. She grabbed Eric's hand and tugged him toward the stairs. "Come on, let's go."

"Leave your bedroom door open," Holly called out as they disappeared.

"Yes, Mom," Lizzy responded with the huffy, longsuffering tone of a teenager.

Holly grinned to herself as she cleared the table and started doing the dishes. What was the fun of having kids if you couldn't torture them in their teenage years?

———

Thirty-five minutes later, Lizzy was flopped on her bed, studying a textbook, but Eric had abandoned prepping for the exam in favor of playing some stupid first-person shooter game on her computer. He sat at her desk, one hand on the cordless mouse, the other clacking away commands on the keyboard, multicolored laser beams exploding various bug-like creatures in chunky red sprays of digitized gore.

Lizzy let him have his fun. After a quick, relatively tame make-out session while her mom washed the dishes downstairs, Eric really had buckled down and done some serious studying. But in typical teenage boy fashion, he eventually lost interest and wandered over to her computer to fire up the game. His textbook, notepad, and cell phone were still on the bed next to her. She glanced at his notes and saw that they were really good, so maybe he figured he had the test nailed and deserved a break.

Or maybe he just finds me boring.

She quickly shook off the thought, getting rid of it before it could even take root. She didn't consider herself one of those insecure, handwringing girls constantly questioning her relationship. She had survived too much in her short lifetime to wallow in doubt and hesitation. Eric had treated her well and been nothing but a top-notch boyfriend. She had absolutely no reason to give sway to negative thoughts about him. Heck, even her mom liked him, and that was saying something, because like all mothers, she could be really overprotective at times. Then again, given all they had been through, a little overprotectiveness was understandable.

Eric's phone buzzed, alerting him that he had a message.

"You got a text," Lizzy said. "Looks like it's from your dad."

"Read it to me." Eric's fingers flashed over the keyboard and the head of some demonic dragon creature on the monitor blew apart in gobs of green goo.

"Your phone's locked, duh. I can see the alert, not the actual text."

"7-7-7-7."

"What?"

"That's my passcode. Punch it in and read me the text, will you?"

"Really?"

"Yeah, sure, what's the problem?"

Lizzy smiled and whatever fleeting concerns she might have been worrying about vanished like dew on a hot summer morning. Clearly Eric trusted her, fully and completely. And as far as Lizzy was concerned, this also meant he really liked her, too. Nobody just gave out their phone password to someone they were just having a casual fling with.

She typed in the code and watched the unlocked phone default to the home screen. She half-expected— okay, hoped—that the wallpaper would be one of their couple photos, but apparently their relationship had not reached that level yet. Instead, Animal from The Muppets stared back at her, clutching drumsticks in one furry fist and making metal horns with the other.

Can't win them all, she chuckled to herself. *And hey, Animal is pretty cool.*

She read the text message out loud to him—his father telling him to pick up some milk, eggs, and coffee creamer on the way home—and resisted the urge to sneak a peek at his other texts or photo library. She figured it was a natural inclination to be nosy and curious, but it would be a betrayal of the trust he had just shown to her. Invading his privacy at the first opportunity would be a dumb move.

Instead, she set the phone down, gave him a warm smile, and went back to studying, basking in the glow and satisfaction of having finally found a guy worth her time and affections.

Downstairs, when she finished cleaning up from supper and putting away the leftovers, Holly flopped down on the couch and turned on the TV. She couldn't hear anything upstairs but that didn't bother her much; she was pretty confident that Lizzy wasn't going to go too far with Eric with her mother lurking nearby. She also didn't think Lizzy would go down that road this early in a relationship anyway. Then again, she had almost given it up to a dumb jock a couple years ago. Hormones could make even a smart girl really stupid in the heat of the moment.

Holly turned the television to one of those entertainment news shows, the kind that served up celebrity gossip with gushing enthusiasm, dishing out cheap paparazzi scoops as if they were the most important thing in the world. She didn't care one single iota about that kind of worthless crap, but it served as background noise that didn't require any focus from her. After pulling a ten-hour shift at the diner followed by a stopover at Stone's house to feed Max and Rocky, she was ready to just sit here and switch her brain off for a few brief moments.

She heard a car turn into her driveway with the familiar crackle of crushed gravel.

Who in the hell...?

She did not get many visitors. Well, actually, she didn't get *any* visitors. While she was generally well-liked in town, she didn't have any close friends. Stone was the only one who ever came to the house, at least until Eric entered their lives.

She glanced at her purse sitting on the counter. It had a Springfield XD-S 9mm pistol in it, magazine maxed out, one in the pipe, and she knew how to use it. She got up and moved the purse to the coffee table, putting it within easier reach. She'd killed a man in this very room once before and she would do it again if she had to.

She brushed aside the curtain but whoever it was, they had already circled around to the front of the house. She heard the screen door to their three-season porch creak open and then close on rusty hinges, followed by the sound of someone knocking on the front door. It was a gentle knock, the light rapping of knuckles rather than the heavy pounding of a fist. It sounded very polite and gentlemanly.

She walked over and looked out the window to see who was standing there. Her heart sank and bile rose in her throat, the acid burn making her want to gag.

It was Deacon White.

Anger surged through her veins as she yanked open the door. "What the hell are you doing at my house, Dave?"

White seemed caught off guard by the door suddenly

flying open and her hostile tone. He recoiled slightly and nervously ran his fingers through his thick mane of dark, gray-flecked hair. "Uh, good evening, Holly. I just...I just thought that maybe we should talk. You know, have a conversation about things?"

"I've got nothing to say to you except leave me the hell alone."

White dropped his hands to his sides and let out a sigh. "May I come in, please?"

"Absolutely not. Whatever it is you think you need to say, you can say it standing right there on my front porch."

"Really, there's no reason to be rude."

"Rude?" Holly scoffed. "You honestly think that I'm the one being rude here? Who's the jackass who doesn't know how to take 'no' for answer?"

"I cannot accept 'no' for an answer when God has clearly informed me that you are the one I'm supposed to marry, that you are supposed to be my wife."

Holly shook her head in disbelief. "Not this *God told me* nonsense again. You really need to let go of that crap."

"It's true. The moment you rolled into Whisper Falls, and I laid eyes on you, the Lord told me that you are the one."

"Yeah, well, maybe you should have a few more chats with God, because He hasn't told me *shit*."

"You can't hear His voice because of Stone," White said. "If it wasn't for that half-heathen cowboy preacher riding into town like Clint Eastwood in *Pale Rider*, you'd know you and I belong together."

"Luke and I are just friends," Holly said. It sounded weak even to her own ears.

"Spare me," White replied.

"It's true."

"Friends who spend an awful lot of time together."

"That's what friendship is."

"It's inappropriate, is what it is," White retorted. "He's a pastor and he should know better."

"Yeah, I don't think Luke agrees with your idea of how a pastor should behave."

"That is the truest thing you have said tonight."

Holly gave him a look that made it clear her patience had expired. "We're done here, David. Time for you to get off my porch, get back in your car, and haul your ass back home."

White smiled thinly. "You know, when you're my wife, you'll need to watch that dirty little mouth of yours. We can't have a deacon's wife going around with a cussing mouth all the time."

"Yeah, but I'll bet there's plenty of other things you're hoping I'll do with my mouth."

The thin smile vanished to be replaced by a frown. "There's no need to be vulgar, Holly."

"Leave, David. Right now. I mean it. Keep stalking me and I'll slap a restraining order on your ass faster than you can blink."

White took a step backward and raised his hands to indicate his compliance. "I'll go," he said. "But Holly, there's simply no running away from God's will. Just open your heart to Him and you'll see that all of Heaven wants us to be together."

Holly shook her head and thought about fetching her gun to get him moving a little faster. "You're a creepy son of a bitch, you know that?"

White retreated another step and actually winked at her. "You're mine, Holly. Nothing can stop it from happening. Not even Lucas Stone." He spun on his heel with military-like precision and walked over to the screen door, where he paused again and said over his shoulder with a little smile, "Don't worry, I'll be in touch."

TEN

BRAXX LANDED in El Paso first. Stone touched down a couple hours later and found his old friend in a hotel lounge, bellied up to the bar, nursing a seltzer water. Braxx shunned alcohol with the ritualistic fervency of a monk. He had never explained why and Stone never asked.

Stone dropped his bag on the floor and slid onto the barstool next to his buddy. He opted for a glass of ice water with a lemon wedge for a hint of citrus flavor. Normally he would have gone with a Jack and Coke, lots of ice, easy on the Jack—a drink that Grizzle, the local bartender back in Whisper Falls, had dubbed "The Preacher," but he never drank on a mission unless he absolutely had to for some reason.

"I see you ordered the hard stuff," he said to Braxx as way of greeting.

Braxx grunted at him. "Says the guy who just ordered a plain glass of water. At least mine has bubbles."

"Yeah, but mine's got a lemon."

"A lemon is what this mission sounds like," said Braxx.

"Having second thoughts? You want to bail, no hard feelings."

Braxx turned his head and gave him a half-grin, half-scowl. "I'd follow you into Hell, you know that. Don't act like I'm some kind of pussy."

"Then what is it?"

"We're not exactly young pups anymore, Luke, and we've both been out of the game awhile."

"Speak for yourself," Stone replied. "I rolled into Whisper Falls and it's like the killing game never stopped."

"You always did have a way of finding trouble," Braxx said. "You're like some kind of shit magnet." He reached up and rubbed at the thin scar above his left eye, a reminder of his near scalping in Syria. "But me, I've just been relaxing, soaking up the sunshine, working on my tan, playing golf, swimming with the dolphins, and enjoying the retired life."

"So, I'll ask again," Stone said. "You want out?"

"Of course not. I'm here, ain't I?" He fidgeted on the stool. "It's just that—"

"Just spit it out, man. We've been friends too long to dance around like this."

"I'm worried about letting you down, all right?" Braxx sighed heavily, as if relieved to have the words out in the open. "You need me to watch your back, but I'm not as good as I used to be. Got some rust on the old skills, you know what I mean?"

"Even if you're only half as good as you used to be, you're better than ninety-five percent of the operators on the planet," Stone replied. "Who gives a shit about a little rust? I mean, you can still shoot straight, right?"

"Straight enough to shoot a flea off a dog's ass at two hundred yards without the dog feeling a thing."

"And you've still got those fancy black belts in karate or ninjitsu or whatever, right?"

"Well, I don't train as hard as I used to, but I could still kick Bruce Lee's butt with one hand tied behind my back and wearing a blindfold."

"Great. You're still a badass. So, stop bitching and get your head in the game." Stone reached over and slapped his friend on the shoulder. "I don't want to turn this into some weird Hallmark moment, but the fact is, there's nobody I'd rather have watching my six than you."

Braxx nodded. "Don't go getting all fucking weepy and shit on me, man. But I appreciate that."

"What's wrong with weeping? Jesus wept, right?"

"Yeah." Braxx nodded and took a sip from his seltzer water. "But Jesus wept because His friend was dead. We're not dead and we're not going to *be* dead. Fuck the Reaper, right? So forget about any weeping and let's kick some ass instead."

"Sounds like a plan."

"So what *is* the plan?" Braxx asked.

"We're meeting Bianca at a bar just over the border in a few hours."

"She agreed to help us?" Braxx sounded surprised.

"She agreed to meet with us," Stone corrected. "Nothing more, nothing less. Still need to sweet talk her into getting us what we need."

"Well, if anyone can sweet talk that spicy little *senorita* into doing something, it's you."

"Don't start your crap."

"Think she's forgiven you yet?"

Stone shrugged. "Guess we'll find out."

Braxx chuckled. "You poor bastard. I'd rather face a hundred cartel cutthroats than that pissed-off hellcat."

"It was a long time ago," Stone said, trying to

convince himself as much as anybody. "I'm sure she's over it by now."

"That's the spirit," Braxx replied. "You just go right ahead and keep on telling yourself that. Far as I'm concerned, you'll be lucky to walk away from Bianca with your balls still intact."

———

Three hours later, they had traded the bar in El Paso for a cantina in Ciudad Acuna on the other side of the International Bridge. The border crossing had gone so easy, laidback, and nonchalant that Stone almost regretted not trying to smuggle weapons into the country. But it had not been a risk worth taking. If caught, they would have been tossed into a Mexican prison faster than a drunk guzzles a bottle of rotgut booze. And while Stone had contacts he could call to get him out of that kind of jam, it might have been days before he was given the chance to make those calls, and by then, the missionaries would probably have been buzzard bait.

No, better to obtain the weapons here. Shouldn't be too hard to get his hands on some hardware, provided Bianca agreed to play ball. Of course, that was no guarantee. Bianca could be volatile and unpredictable, especially where Stone was concerned.

They sat at a tall table in the corner beneath a painting of a matador stabbing a bull. Stone faced the door while Braxx kept an eye on the emergency exit in the back in case trouble came calling from that direction. Again, when it came to Bianca, anything was possible. They had both ordered beers to keep from drawing too much attention to themselves—gringos at a cantina but not drinking would raise eyebrows—but neither had touched a drop, refusing to have their senses and reactions dulled even slightly by alcohol consumption. Condensation trickled down the bottles and soaked into the cork coasters designed to prevent water rings on a table already stained with dozens of them.

Stone removed his Stetson and sleeved sweat from his forehead. If the air conditioner was working in here, it sure as hell didn't feel like it. He'd been in saunas that felt cooler than this. Even this late at night, the temperature stayed hot and muggy this time of year. The beer was growing more tempting by the minute, even though it was probably barely above room temperature by now.

The door opened and a stunning Latina woman with the kind of supermodel looks that belonged on a Hollywood runway strutted in like she owned the place. As she glided through the cantina, threading her way among the small crowd of patrons, every male eye—and more than a few female ones—shifted in her direction. No surprise, because the woman had killer curves in all the right places, jeans tight on legs and hips, breasts swelling the silk blouse that showed ample, sweat-beaded cleavage. Only when the patrons met her gaze and saw the dark, glittering danger lurking deep in those smoke-hued eyes did everyone quickly turn away.

Everyone except Stone. He kept his eyes fixed right on her, watching for a gun or a knife to appear. Hell, maybe both, knowing her. He wouldn't put it past her to stick a blade in his ribs for an appetizer and put a bullet in his head for the main course.

She sashayed right up to him with a wide smile on her face, lips devil-red and parted just enough to offer a glimpse of perfect white teeth, and said, "Hello, Lucas. Been a long time."

Stone dialed his tension back a notch. Looked like she wasn't going to gut him right here after all. "Good to see you again, Bianca."

The smile vanished so fast it was like a magic trick. Her right hand swept up and around so that her open palm slapped against his face with a flesh-on-flesh cracking sound so loud, even Braxx winced. A left hook followed hot on its heels and her knuckles smashed against his jaw. Stone could have easily blocked both blows but in some ways, he had it coming, and figured it was best to let her get it out of her system.

Her right fist shot out again, this time slamming into his solar plexus. Stone let out a small groan and he wasn't faking. For such a slender woman, she could really hit. Or maybe it was just years of pent-up rage giving her blows an extra edge.

Bianca blew a strand of black hair out of her eyes and pasted the smile back on her face. "Good to see you again too, Lucas."

As Stone rubbed his aching jaw, Braxx looked at Bianca and said, "If you're all done with the foreplay, can I get you a drink?"

"Done?" Bianca arched her eyebrows. "I'm just getting started with this *rompecorazones*."

"I have no fucking idea what that means," Braxx said.

"Look it up."

"Sure, maybe someday, if I get really, really bored. You want a drink or not?"

"Don't bother." Bianca grabbed the bottle of lukewarm beer in front of Stone, raised it to her lips, and chugged it down without pausing before slamming the empty bottle down on the table. "I'll just take his. He owes me."

"That works," Braxx said. "Luke, can I get you another beer so the little lady here can steal it from you?"

Stone waved him off. "After that punch to the gut she just gave me, I don't think I could drink anything anyway."

Bianca made a derisive chuffing noise. "You're one to talk about a gut punch after what you did to me." She slid onto the empty chair to Stone's right. "Made me fall in love with you and then broke my heart." Her dark eyes narrowed, piercing him. "Tell me, Lucas, was it even real, what we had? Or was I just some fuck-and-chuck fling to you?"

"Whoa! Language," Braxx interjected. "I may look like a tough guy, but I've got the ears of a nun and the delicate sensibilities of a virgin. Don't make me blush."

Bianca shot him a sideways glance. "Don't make me hurt you, *pringado*."

"Great," Braxx muttered. "Another word I need to look up."

Bianca refocused her attention on Stone. "I want an answer, Lucas."

"I'm not here to talk about the past," Stone said.

"You'll talk about it, or you won't get any help from me. Simple as that. You owe me explanations."

Stone sighed, knowing there was no way to dodge this conversation, much as he would have liked to. "It was a long time ago, Bianca. I was young and stupid."

"Not as stupid as me for believing your bullshit and hopping into bed with you."

Stone struggled to find the right words and his silent prayers for help seemed to be going unanswered. Apparently, even God found it amusing to watch him squirm. *Thanks, Lord.*

"It was real enough," he finally said. "We were working closely together at the time and sparks happened. I wasn't just using you, if that's what you think."

Braxx interjected. "Just so I can kinda-sorta-maybe follow along while you two jacked-up lovebirds hash out old wounds, can someone refresh my memory of what was going on back then?"

"I'm a DEA agent stationed in Mexico," Bianca explained. "Lucas was on loan to a DEA task force created to tackle cartel violence along the border. I was his contact."

Braxx gave Stone a look. "I'm guessing you just sat behind a desk and pushed paperwork, right?"

"Something like that, yeah."

"Call it what it was," Bianca said. "You were an assassin, a sicario."

"My kills were sanctioned."

"That doesn't change what I just said."

"You didn't have a problem with me pulling the trigger back then."

"And I don't have a problem with it now, either," Bianca replied. "But while you were busy putting crosshairs on targets, you also put your crosshairs on me."

"Don't be so dramatic," Stone said irritably. "And while you're at it, don't play the victim. You knew exactly what you were doing."

"Of course I knew what I was doing. I wasn't some virgin nun. But what I *didn't* know was that when you were done stacking bodies and headed back to wherever the hell you came from, you would also be done with me." She leaned forward, angry fire burning hot in her eyes. "I loved you, Lucas Stone, and you made me feel used."

"For that, I'm sorry," Stone said, and meant it. "I never wanted to hurt you, but there was no way things were going to work out between us."

"Guess we'll never know."

Braxx shook his head and muttered, "You two need to

go find a bathroom stall and have a grudge fuck or some makeup sex, and I'm not sure which."

"You're not helping, Braxx," Stone growled.

"Actually, I think it would help a lot."

"Shut up."

Bianca ignored Braxx, her eyes locked on Stone like a drone pilot getting ready to fire a missile. She studied him, saying nothing for several long heartbeats, then—"I believe you."

"About what?" Stone asked.

"You said you're sorry. I believe you."

"So you accept my apology?"

"I accept it," Bianca said. "But let's not get all confused about where things stand between us. Acceptance and forgiveness are not the same thing."

"One step at a time, I guess," said Stone.

"Thank God that's over with," Braxx muttered. "Listening to you two bitch at each other was like watching porn that never gets to the point."

"It was, like, five minutes," Stone retorted.

"That's four minutes too long," said Braxx. "Now, can we get down to business? In case you forgot, the clock is ticking."

"You told me the barebones version on the phone," Bianca said to Stone. "Give me the details."

Stone quickly and matter-of-factly relayed everything he knew about the situation and let her watch the crucifixion/ransom demand video he had forwarded from Andy's phone to his. She viewed it without flinching, but Stone saw the muscles in her jaw tighten when the nails were hammered home.

"So, what do you need from me?" Bianca asked when it finished playing.

"Weapons, for starters," Stone replied. "And I'm

hoping you can work some magic and get a lead on where the missionaries are being held. I'm assuming you still have contacts all over the country."

"You can assume whatever you like," she replied. "What kind of weapons are we talking about?"

Braxx pulled a piece of paper from his pocket and passed it across the table to her. "Nothing too crazy," he said. "Pistols, rifles, ammo, and explosives, mostly."

"That's it? Sure you don't want me to rustle up an A-10 Warthog or Apache chopper for you?"

"Nah," Braxx replied. "We're saving those for next time."

"Don't be so sure there will *be* a next time," Bianca said. "If my mood doesn't improve, I may kill you myself before you get out of the country."

"Hey," Braxx protested. "What the hell? I thought you said you were good to go."

Bianca ignored him and studied the list. "These won't be all that hard to obtain. But finding the whereabouts of your missionaries might require me to grease some palms." She looked at Stone. "I assume you brought some palm grease?"

"I've got plenty of cash, both American dollars and pesos. Didn't figure I was getting the guns or information for free."

"That church reimbursing you for the costs of this little rescue mission?"

"That church can barely afford pizza for youth group," Stone said. "I'm bankrolling this operation with my own funds."

Bianca smirked. "That part of your redemption arc?"

"What's that supposed to mean?"

"You earned your money doing the devil's work for all those years," she replied. "Knowing you, I'm guessing that using that money to save some of God's children is your way of trying to tip the scales back toward the righteous side."

"Like I said before, everything I did back then was sanctioned."

"That doesn't mean you don't have some *culpa,* some guilt."

"Less than you might think, but yeah, I wasn't always dancing with the angels back then."

Bianca waved a hand as if his words meant nothing to her and hell, they probably didn't. "So, you've got money. Good for you. But money isn't going to cover *my* fee."

"Your fee?" Braxx echoed. "You mean you're not going to help us out of the goodness of your heart?" He rolled his eyes so hard he probably saw the back of his skull. "Now there's a shocker."

"My good heart got broken beyond repair by this *hijo de puta* a long time ago," Bianca retorted, voice laced with bitterness. She smiled at Stone, a smile that was one part seductress, one part cold-blooded shark. "Now I want something for my service."

"And what's that?" Stone asked.

"I want you in my bed again."

Stone was dumbfounded. She could have said that she wanted him to move the Great Pyramid to Alaska and he wouldn't have been more shocked.

Braxx let out a half-snort, half-laugh. "Holy shit, the plot thickens. Little Miss Broken Heart here's still got a hankering for some of that special Lucas Stone lovin'."

Stone swallowed hard, mind racing. "You can't be serious."

"Oh, I'm dead serious," Bianca assured him. She leaned forward, and whether by design or by accident, the movement pushed up her breasts and accentuated her cleavage. Stone got a good look and did his damnedest to suppress the carnal memories the sight stirred up. "I have had plenty of lovers since you left me, Lucas, but none of them made me feel the way you did. Despite how things ended, there was something special between us while it lasted."

"Bianca, listen to me…"

She kept on talking, her words rolling right over whatever protestation he wanted to make. "I want to feel that again, Lucas. Take me to bed, make love to me one more time the way you used to. Make me feel something I have not felt since you walked out of my life without so much as a backward glance." Her eyelids drooped half-closed as if savoring her own sweet memories. "Do that for me, and I will help you find your precious missionaries. That is my price. Take it or leave it."

Braxx was grinning like an idiot. "How will you be paying, sir? Cash, card, or cock?"

Stone shot him a glaring look that said, *I'm gonna kill you when this is over.* Braxx appeared unfazed by the tacit threat and kept on grinning, clearly amused by Stone's discomfort.

He turned back to Bianca, who was staring at him with impenetrable eyes, making it impossible to decipher exactly what she was thinking at the moment. "Bianca, listen, I can't do that. You know I can't."

She smiled, grabbed a napkin, jotted down an address, and slid it over to him. "Meet me there in one hour and give me what I asked for. If not, you'll never see me again and good luck with your missionaries." She leaned forward even further, giving Stone a full look down her shirt and all the pleasures that awaited there, and softly said, "It's not like I'm asking you to do something you've never done before."

With that, she slid off her chair and exited the cantina with the same self-assured, hip-swaying swagger she had entered.

———

"What the hell am I going to do?" Stone asked. Bianca had been gone for ten minutes and it was about the tenth time he had voiced that question.

"Gotta admit," Braxx said, "I did not see this twist coming." He paused, and then added, "Maybe suggesting you grudge fuck her in the bathroom wasn't such bad advice after all."

"You're not helping."

"I would have guarded the door for you guys, made sure nobody interrupted the reunion. I had thirty seconds to spare, no problem."

"Braxx," Stone growled in a warning tone.

His buddy held up his hands in a surrender gesture. "All right, okay, fine, I'll stop busting your nuts." Pause. "Because that's what Bianca wants you to do in about forty-five minutes." He chortled at his own joke.

"God, I hate you sometimes," Stone muttered. "You know you can be a real ass, right?"

"Remember, I'm laughing with you, not at you."

"The hell you are." Stone rubbed his temples, sighed, and again asked, "What the hell am I going to do?"

"I don't want to state the obvious, but you could just give her what she wants," Braxx pointed out.

"That's not gonna happen." Stone shook his head emphatically. "I'm not sleeping with her."

"You already did."

"I'm not sleeping with her *again*."

Braxx shrugged. "Your call, amigo. But if you leave her hanging, these missionaries of yours might very well be up shit creek without the proverbial paddle. Are their deaths worth keeping your dick dry?"

Stone gave him a look. "Listen, I'm not supposed to be the only one with morals here."

Another shrug from Braxx. "This is one of those times where maybe you have to do something wrong in order to do something good. It sucks, but life ain't always clean."

"What if it was you she wanted? Would you do it?"

"Of course not. I'm married."

"Yeah? What about Holly?"

"What about her?" Braxx asked. "She's just a friend, right? That's what you keep telling me. You two aren't even dating, for god's sake, so it's not like you're cheating on her. Besides, she never needs to know. What happens in Mexico stays in Mexico."

Stone shook his head, smirked, and gave his friend a look of mock disapproval. "You're a terrible Christian, you know that?"

"Maybe," Braxx conceded. "Or maybe I'm just a pragmatic one who knows that sometimes life gets dirty, and we have to do things that go against our better angels in order to get the job done."

"Sinning in the name of righteousness," Stone said. He almost slapped a scoffing edge onto the words but caught himself at the last second as he realized how hypocritical he was being. He was a vigilante, a person who punished outside the boundaries of the law when he felt primal justice was deserved. What Braxx was suggesting he do wasn't any worse than that. What was some brief fornication compared to a whole bunch of killing? Nothing, really.

Still, Stone didn't think he could do it.

He threw some money down on the table to cover the

beers and got ready to leave. "Stay here," he told Braxx. "I won't be long."

"To bang or not to bang, that is the question," Braxx said. "So, what are you going to do?"

"Hell if I know," Stone replied, and walked out into the humid night.

ELEVEN

HOLLY HAD no way of knowing if Stone was thinking about her, but she was definitely thinking about him.

Eric had left about an hour ago, politely thanking her for letting him come over. Lizzy was now barricaded in her room doing whatever teenagers did when they retreated to their personal sanctuaries. Rotting her brain by mindlessly scrolling TikTok or YouTube was a distinct possibility but knowing Lizzy, she was more likely reading a book. The girl had eclectic taste in literature. You could find everything from Don Pendelton potboilers to Stephen King doorstoppers to classics by Tolstoy or the works of the ancient historian Josephus on her shelves.

Holly had exchanged her work clothes for thin, lightweight silk pajamas that did their best to keep the heat off her skin. The old house did not have central air but a portable A/C unit hummed away in the room's only window, stripping away the humidity and cooling the temperature to tolerable levels.

She slid her legs under the covers and propped herself up into a sitting position by stuffing pillows between her back and the headboard. As she thumbed through her texts and saw the last one from Stone, letting her know he had landed in El Paso, she felt a pang of longing and couldn't help but wish he was here with her. *We have got to stop dancing around our feelings,* she thought. *Life's too short to guard your heart forever.*

Despite what that internal voice was telling her, she still tried to deny her emotions, tried to shove them back down into the long-locked compartment in which she kept them, buried like some forgotten treasure, never to be dug up. But the truth was, she ached for him. Despite her halfhearted attempt at denial, deep down she knew that if he were here right now, she would be inviting him into bed with her. The silk pajamas would be forgotten on the floor as they consummated what they so clearly felt.

She threw the covers off. Damn, it was getting hot in here. She chuckled to herself. *Girl, that cowboy preacher has got you all hot and bothered and acting like a hussy tonight.*

She sent him a short good night text, waited several minutes, and quelled a bit of disappointment when there was no response. He had been very clear that he would most likely be out of contact during the rescue mission.

She set her phone down on the nightstand and turned off the light. Her eyes had just started to adjust to the darkness when the phone chimed, alerting her to an incoming text. She smiled and reached for the phone. She would sleep better tonight having heard from him before going to bed.

She read the message, and the smile turned to a frown.

It wasn't from Stone.

She didn't recognize the number, and the text was obscene enough to belong in a hardcore porno magazine, describing in excruciatingly graphic detail what the mysterious sender wanted to do to her sexually. The violator described her body—or rather, how they imagined her body—in salacious terms and not a single inch went untouched. No position went unmentioned, no deviant act got left out. By the time she reached the end of the seemingly unending message—seriously, it must have taken forever to type—the sender had spelled out everything they wanted to do to her, from normative to kinky to downright twisted and sadistic. Some of the things described would have made the Marquis de Sade blush.

The shock wore off quickly, immediately replaced by burning anger. A nerve in her jaw throbbed hotly as she clenched her teeth. She had zero doubt who had sent her this nasty, filthy shit.

Deacon David White.

She didn't bother responding to the text. The sick pervert didn't deserve a response. She just slammed the phone down on the nightstand again, almost hard enough to crack the protective case, and laid in the dark, seething mad. She knew White was obsessed with her—his appearance at her door tonight had made that clear, if she hadn't known it already—but this was pretty goddamned low. Lower than she had ever expected the head deacon to go. Maybe her continual rejection had made him snap. Not that it mattered. There was no excuse, no justification, for the obscenities he had sent her.

She would deal with him tomorrow. She prayed to God that he came into the Birch Bark for breakfast. He would be lucky if she didn't pour hot coffee all over his crotch before slapping his face and telling him what a sick piece of shit he was.

She went to sleep dreaming of knocking the bastard's teeth out with a frying pan.

———

Down the hall in her bedroom, Lizzy heard her mother slam down her phone and wondered what in the world that was about. Mom didn't usually get that worked up and even when she did, she rarely took that anger out on her expensive electronics. Wasn't like they were rolling in money and could easily replace smashed devices. Hopefully it wasn't bad news about Stone.

She didn't want to let her mind go down that dark path, so she picked up her own phone and texted Eric. **Mom's pissed about something.** Unlike most kids her age, Lizzy actually believed in proper grammar and punctuation while texting. She'd read an article somewhere that those things were now considered "white privilege," but she didn't care. She saw no reason to sound dumb. Eric teased her about it all the time, but she couldn't let it go.

U know whut? he texted back. Unlike Lizzy, Eric never bothered with trivial things like spelling. She was actually surprised he had bothered to add the question mark at the end.

Her thumbs danced across the keyboard on her phone. **No idea.**

Could it be bout us?

No, she would've said something to me.

Thnk she herd us makin out?

Lizzy felt her face flush, but she wasn't sure why. What the hell was wrong with her? They were seventeen, not seven, and Eric had taken a purity vow to maintain his virginity until marriage, so making out was about as far as things were going to go. She texted a reply: *No way. She would have been up those stairs faster than greased lightning.*

A laughing emoji popped up on her screen, followed by: **Its not 1884 ya know. Nobody sez greased lightning anymore.**

She sent him a frowning emoji and chased it with: **I do. You're supposed to say it makes me sound cute.**

Eric texted back, **U R cute. Send me sum sexy pix.**

No way. I told you, no nudes.

Not nudes. Just sumthin sexy.

All fun & games until your dad sees them.

Ill delete em b4 I go 2 sleep. Promise.

Lizzy shook her head and let a little smile play across her lips. He must be all worked up. He was really pushing hard tonight. She had always stuck to her guns and refused to supply him with any pictures of her not fully clothed, not even a swimsuit photo. But maybe tonight she would ease off the restrictions and give him a little treat. He'd earned it with how good his deep-kissing had been earlier.

She texted: **Stand by.**

He responded with a heart-eyes emoji followed by several exclamation points to symbolize his excitement.

After making sure her bedroom door was closed and locked—couldn't have her mom catch her doing this or she'd be grounded for life!—she stripped down to her bra and panties and quickly snapped a half-dozen photos from different angles, doing her best to give him "good" angles while also trying to remain somewhat tasteful. She wasn't sure she struck the right balance, but whatever. Wasn't like Eric was going to complain.

She took a few moments to apply some soft-focus filters to the pictures, giving them a classier—in her mind, anyway—vibe. She was already starting to regret her decision, but a promise was a promise. He had trusted her with his phone passcode, so she needed to return the favor and trust him when he said he would delete the photos. Before she could change her mind and disappoint him, she texted him the photographs. Almost immediately, the "Delivered" notification appeared beneath them.

She chewed on her lower lip as she waited for his response.

Less than a minute later, he texted: **Holy cow! These R awesum! UR smokin hot, grl**. He had tacked a fire emoji on to the end.

Lizzy smiled to herself at his reaction, but she already felt something cold and unpleasant slithering around in her guts. It took her a few heartbeats to recognize the sensation as a clammy mixture of guilt, shame, and regret. What had she been thinking? She knew better. Sure, she trusted Eric, but plenty of girls had trusted guys who had then shared their inappropriate photos with their friends or posted them on social media for the whole world to see. Half the girls in her school had stories like that. Sometimes it seemed like having your photos leaked had almost become a rite of passage.

Even as Eric texted, **Thnx 4 the pix. Nite. Luv U**, Lizzy buried her face in her hands with only one thought going through her mind.

Oh my God, what have I done?

TWELVE

STONE MIGHT HAVE BEEN out of the black ops game for years, but he still recognized a safehouse when he saw one. Clearly the address Bianca had written on the napkin was not her private residence. This place was too plain, too nondescript, void of any personality. And while it wasn't exactly in a bad part of town, the area wasn't upscale enough for someone with Bianca's income. She most likely just crashed here when she was working a case, meeting an informant, or hiding a witness.

Stone really didn't care. The designated meeting place could have been the Taj Mahal and he wouldn't have given a rat's ass. He just wanted to get this over with and get back to the business of rescuing the missionaries. Being forced to dance to Bianca's tune was starting to irritate him. Innocent people were being held captive and crucified while she busied herself playing games as some twisted way of dealing with her broken heart from long ago.

But right now, he didn't have any other options, so he was forced to indulge her fuckery, to let her pull the strings and jerk him around like some kind of helpless marionette. But the second he had what he needed—weapons and intel—he planned on slashing those strings to ribbons.

He knocked on the door and it opened almost immediately, as if she had been waiting for him. She yanked him inside, slammed the door closed, and threw herself at him with something disturbingly close to desperation. Her arms wrapped around his neck like a living noose and her lips pressed against his while her voluptuous body writhed against him with wanton hunger.

"Bianca, wait—" he started to say, but he couldn't finish the words because the moment he opened his mouth to speak, her tongue invaded, hot and wet, sliding deep as she murmured a passionate moan into his throat.

One of her hands slid down his back and grabbed his ass, fingers digging hard, pulling him tight against her. Despite his willpower and resistance, he was still a man, and his body responded accordingly, involuntarily, his flesh betraying his emotional wishes. Bianca seemed to take this as a sign of his acceptance and started grinding even harder.

It had been a long time but there was still a familiarity between them. Her movements rekindled memories of lovemaking from their brief time together. She had been a wild, generous lover, no doubt about that. Against Stone's better judgment, he felt temptation taking root, the devil in his heart telling him to unshackle his inhibitions and just enjoy the pleasure of the moment. After all, it was for the greater good, right? He needed Bianca's help to secure weapons and get a fix on the missionaries' location and she would not give him that help unless he first gave her what she wanted, satisfied her carnal needs, and brought some kind of closure to their past. It was the perfect justification.

Just imagine it's Holly, not Bianca, the devilish voice whispered. *Maybe that'll make it better for you.*

Bianca broke their embrace just long enough to tear open her blouse. Stone watched her fingers work, exposing more tantalizing skin with every button that popped loose. The bra beneath was black lace and beads of sweat trickled down her cleavage as mapping out a path for his lips. Stone knew it was wrong—what the hell was he doing?—but he couldn't tear his eyes away from Bianca's frenzied striptease.

It's been so damn long, he thought. *I haven't been with a woman since Theresa. Wrong or not, I need this.*

Bianca surged against him again, pressing, writhing, grinding. Her breasts flattened against his chest, warm and promising. His temptation kicked up several notches. Bianca seemed to sense he was right on the edge of surrender. "Do it," she whispered in his ear, breath hot on his skin, tongue dancing along his lobe. "Take me. Make love to me. Make me feel what we used to feel. Just one last time, Lucas."

Her hand slid between their bodies, reaching for his belt buckle, grazing against the zipper. They were nearing the point of no return.

Somehow, Stone found the strength to push her back. "I can't," he said, holding her at arm's length. "Bianca, I'm sorry, but...I just can't."

She stood a foot away, dark eyes flashing with heat and danger, chest heaving, her sweat-dappled breasts begging him to reconsider. His hands were on her shoulders, but she knocked them away. "You're telling me no?" She sounded like she could not believe it. "You're *denying* me?"

"I have to."

"You want me. Don't even try to deny it. Your body is

giving you away." She reached for the front of his pants, which were still uncomfortably tight.

He shifted away from her. "I'm the master of my body, not the other way around."

"If you're the *maestro*, then tell it to give me what I want."

Stone shook his head. "Sorry, but I can't do that." The fog of lust and passion was receding from his mind. He felt in control again, temptation subdued, the devil back on a leash. Talk about a close call.

"You can't do that?" Bianca echoed and then cocked her head to the side. "Even if it means all those missionaries will be killed?"

"I'm not giving up my morals, not even for the greater good," Stone said. "I'll just have to trust that God will show me another way to save the people I came here for."

Bianca still had not buttoned her blouse, letting it hang open, half falling off her shoulders, the invitation there, as if there might still be a chance he would change his mind and take what she was offering. "Tell me why," she said. "Tell me why you don't want to be with me."

"Simple," Stone replied. "I don't believe in sex without love."

Bianca scoffed. "Yeah, right."

"It's the truth."

"You did before. Pretty sure it wasn't love on your mind the first time you screwed me after that tequila binge."

Stone inwardly winced at the memory. "That was a long time ago. Things change. People change. *I* changed."

She studied him an intense, piercing stare that seemed to carve right through him and lay open his secrets. "You love someone else, don't you." It wasn't phrased as a question.

Stone answered anyway. "It's complicated. But yes, there's someone else."

Hurt and disappointment flickered across her eyes. Stone continued to be stunned that a brief, torrid fling so many years ago could still impact her this much. Proof that you could never be sure what kinds of wounds you would sustain when it came to matters of the heart, nor how slowly those wounds would take to become scars.

Bianca sighed heavily. "All right, Lucas, have it your way." She buttoned up her blouse. "Clearly things *have* changed, as you say. It would appear you are a good man now." She chuckled throatily. "Who would have thought such a thing possible?"

"I wouldn't go so far as to say I'm a good man," Stone admitted. "But I'm trying to be better than I was."

"Looking for redemption, right?"

"Something like that, I guess."

She stepped forward and for a moment, Stone thought she was making another advance. But she just stood on her toes, kissed him softly on the cheek, and said, "I respect a man who sticks to his beliefs, especially when it might cost him."

Thinking of the missionaries, Stone looked her in the eyes and asked, "Is it going to cost me, Bianca? I want you to think about the innocent lives at stake."

"You don't need to plead your case," she said. "I made my play—you can't blame a heartbroken *chica* for trying, right? And you shot me down for reasons I fully understand. I'm not going to let your missionaries die just because you refused my bed."

"Thanks for that."

"I'll arrange a meeting with some gun dealers so you and Braxx can obtain weapons for your little fiesta."

"Are they reliable?"

Bianca shrugged. "They're black market arms dealers. Are any of them reliable?"

"Point taken."

Bianca moved away from the door and walked into the living room area where she plucked her cell phone off the coffee table. Stone leaned against the wall and folded his arms across his chest while he waited for her to work her magic.

Whoever she called, the conversation was short, cryptic, and conducted in Spanish so rapid-fire that Stone barely followed twenty-five percent of what they were saying, despite having a passable grasp of the language. When she ended the call, less than sixty seconds had passed.

"That was fast," Stone commented.

Bianca smirked at him. "Some girls like it that way from time to time."

Stone shook his head. "Don't start."

She kept smirking and said, "You're no fun anymore. But we've already established that." She rattled off an address, which he repeated several times, committing it to memory. "That's a warehouse where Carlito does business."

"Carlito's the dealer, I assume?"

Bianca nodded. "And the warehouse is his chop shop."

"Thought you said he was a gun dealer?"

"Carlito has his fingers in a lot of pies."

Stone arched an eyebrow. "Yours?"

"Jealous?"

"No, just asking."

She shook her head. "Don't insult me."

"Sorry."

"He'll meet you there at midnight. You can be sure he'll have backup with him."

"How many?"

"At least four guys," she replied. "Maybe more."

"He'll have what we need?"

"Carlito could get you a suitcase nuke if you had the cash and the patience."

"Sounds like the kind of guy we should be taking out, not doing business with," Stone muttered.

"Desperate times make for strange bedfellows, right?"

"I suppose," Stone conceded.

Bianca's eyes narrowed. "You're a killer, Lucas. You were back then, and I can tell you still are. So don't get all high and mighty. You may have found God, but anyone who knows you can tell that you've still got some devil in you. How many laws have you already broken on this rescue mission? How many more are you going to break before it's all said and done? And you and I both know that you're going to kill a whole lot of people in the next twenty-four hours. You may consider them righteous kills but in the eyes of the law—both Mexican laws and American laws—those kills will count as cold-blooded murder. So maybe you shouldn't be so quick to sneer at others who are living outside the law as well."

Her words had bite, but Stone refused to let the fangs dig in too deep. There was a big difference between breaking the law in the name of a greater good and breaking the law solely for profit. But this wasn't the time or the place—nor was he in the mood—to argue with her, so he simply said, "I see your point."

"Of course you do," Bianca replied. "You're many things, but a hypocrite was never one of them."

"We're all hypocrites in some way."

She rolled her eyes. "Look at you, getting all philosophical. You really know how to turn a woman on."

"Just keeping it real."

"You're way too serious these days. You were more

fun back then." Without waiting for a response, she said, "All right, back to business. How did you get here?"

"Drove the rental. Left Braxx at the bar."

"Poor guy. He doesn't even drink."

"Yeah, but he pretends real well. He'll be fine."

She reached into a decorative ceramic bowl on the coffee table, pulled out a set of keys, and tossed them to him. "There's an SUV parked in the garage. Clean plates and registration that won't come back to you if this mission goes sideways, which there's at least a fifty-fifty chance it will. Put your rental in the garage until this is over and we can assess any damage that needs mitigating. That happens, I'll run whatever interference I can. While you and Braxx go meet with Carlito and get yourselves kitted up, I'll make some calls and try to get a bead on where the missionaries might be. Hopefully I'll have a lead or two by the time you get back."

"Thanks, Bianca. I appreciate all the help."

"Don't thank me too much, Lucas. As far as I'm concerned, you owe me one—*more* than one—and somewhere down the road, you can bet your *culo* I'm going to call in the favor."

Stone nodded. "Fair enough. I do owe you and I won't forget it."

"I'll hold you to that, *amante*."

I have no doubt you will, Stone thought, but kept it to himself.

THIRTEEN

MY GOD, *my God, why have You forsaken me?*

The words rose unbidden in Amber's mind, floating up from a dark place in her soul. Though she knew that her current suffering did not even come close to what Christ endured on the cross, her cry to God was the same lament Jesus uttered as He hung there. Because that's how she felt right now—abandoned by the God she had dedicated her life to serving.

She was sitting on the cold dirt of what appeared to be a horse stall, her back against the rear wall, feet stretched out in front of her toward the door. Both her wrists and ankles remained flex-cuffed tight enough to interfere with circulation and cause some serious discomfort. But she had not even bothered complaining, knowing it would be useless. The guards that roamed the barn, occasionally leering at her through the bars in the stall door, would just ignore her cries or, worse, sever her tongue.

So she sat and suffered and wondered where God was in all this. The question of why a holy, loving, all-powerful Creator allowed evil things to happen was a question all believers wrestled with from time to time, but for Amber, it had never felt so personal. Until now, it had been nothing more than a sermon topic, an interesting theological debate to kick around with the congregation during the Sunday morning post-communion coffee hour. Have a donut, ponder the mystery and enigma of the Almighty.

Now, as she huddled in the dirt, hostage to a violent madman, mourning the brutal death of her friend Jack Spurgeon, and scared out of her mind about what would happen next—not just to her, but to all of them—the question of why God allowed the saints to suffer was very, very real.

She knew the others were locked in nearby stalls as well. They had tried talking to each other, but the guards had demanded their silence and they had complied; again, the repeated threats to cut out their tongues remained a constant worry. But Amber caught the occasional stifled sob or muffled whimper and knew she was not alone in this hell she was enduring. She tried to take some small measure of comfort in that but found it impossible. Bill, Claudia, Dianne, Gary—they were all here because of her. If possible, she would have gladly sacrificed her own life if it meant the others could return home safely.

She heard footsteps outside the stall door. When she lifted her head, Armando Ochoa was staring at her through the bars. No evil grin, no lecherous glint in his eyes, just an impassive gaze that gave away nothing of the man's thoughts. But Amber had already seen enough to know that his thoughts were dark and demented, possibly even demonic. For surely nobody would nail priests and missionaries to a cross unless they were possessed by the devil himself.

After staring at her for several long, unblinking

moments, Ochoa's face finally cracked into a smirk. "Are you enjoying your accommodations, *senorita*?"

"I've had worse." Amber refused to give him the satisfaction of acknowledging her discomfort. As resistance went, it wasn't much, but it was all she had.

"I think that is a lie," said Ochoa. "I believe you have always enjoyed the comfort of a warm bed at night, clean sheets, a soft pillow under your pretty little head. Not cold dirt and the smell of pig shit."

"You don't know me," Amber retorted. His words were true but she wasn't going to tell him that.

Ochoa leaned closer, pressing his face against the iron bars. "I will know everything there is to know about you, *puta*, if your husband does not pay me. Five hundred thousand or I will know the taste of your mouth, the touch of your skin, all the pleasures of your flesh. I will know what it feels like to crush you beneath me, to take from you that which you would never freely give to someone like me."

Amber closed her eyes, unable to repress the shudder that ran through her at the thought of being violated by this hulking madman.

Ochoa chuckled, low and vile. "When I take you, your eyes will be open, that I promise you. You will look me in the eyes as I fuck you to death before feeding your ravaged body to the pigs and if you do not, I will slice off your eyelids."

Amber opened her eyes and quietly said, "I have done nothing to you."

"As I have said, you are paying for the sins of others who came before you." Ochoa stepped back from the stall door. "But do not worry about it just yet, *Senorita* Lillegard. Your time may come, but it is not tonight. Tonight, I will choose someone else for my pleasure."

She heard his footsteps as he moved down the line of stalls. A moment later she heard him say, "This one."

"No, no, no...please, no."

Amber recognized Dianne Fitzgerald's terrified voice, her horrified pleas.

"NO! NO! PLEASE! LEAVE ME ALONE!"

Amber squeezed her eyes shut, trembling, praying. *Lord, don't let this happen. Please don't let this happen. I'm begging You.*

A sharp *crack!* The harsh sound of flesh striking flesh. Dianne gasped as the vicious slap turned her cries to whimpers.

Do something!

Amber opened her eyes, took a deep breath, summoned every shred of courage she had left in her soul, and shouted, "Take me!"

Footsteps approached and a moment later, Ochoa's face reappeared at the barred window of her stall. "What did you say?"

"Take me," Amber repeated. Fear pounded through her veins, but she was determined to push through it. "Instead of Dianne, take me. I'll go with you. Please, just leave her alone."

Ochoa's eyes narrowed to glittering slits. "What kind of game are you playing at?"

"No game." Amber shook her head. "I just...I just don't want you to...to hurt her."

"So, you're willing to let me hurt you instead? You will take her place?"

Amber swallowed hard and nodded.

Ochoa stared at her, then broke out in a big, teeth-flashing grin. "You Christians," he said. "All about the sacrifice, like it makes you noble or something."

Amber raised her face, chin thrust forward defiantly. "If Christ sacrificed Himself for me, I can sacrifice myself for her." She could feel strength and courage pouring through her from depths she had not known she possessed. Clearly her prayer for help had been answered.

"Sorry, *senorita*, but you will not be sacrificing yourself for anyone tonight," Ochoa said. "I am saving you for later. Mrs. Fitzgerald, your beloved sister in *Cristo*, will have to supply my entertainment this evening."

Amber trembled but tried not to let it show, not wanting to give him the satisfaction. But she feared the horrors Dianne was about to endure would break her beyond all repair. The woman was strong in the faith, but truth be told, weak in spirit. Her body might survive the imminent abuse, but her sanity surviving intact was questionable.

Dear God, don't let her break. Give her the strength that can only come from You.

"Nothing else to say?" Ochoa asked with a mocking sneer.

"I won't waste my words or my breath on a monster like you," Amber snapped. "You can go to hell."

Ochoa's sneer widened. "I look forward to breaking you, *senorita*. When your time comes, you will most definitely 'waste' your breath on me, because you will need it to scream."

Amber said nothing more and Ochoa walked away. Moments later, Dianne started pleading again as she was taken from the stall and dragged out of the barn. A few minutes later, coming from the direction of the house, her anguished screams tore through the night. They lasted a long time.

An hour or so after she was taken, Dianne was hauled back to the barn and returned to her stall. She didn't make a sound, not so much as a whimper or a sob. Amber tried talking to her despite the guards' warnings but got no response. Maybe Dianne was unconscious and if so, that was a mercy.

Or maybe being brutalized had broken her soul.

With nobody watching her at that particular moment and therefore no need to put on a strong, defiant face, Amber let tears spill from her eyes and slide down her cheeks. Dianne's body and soul weren't the only broken things in this barn. Amber felt her faith fraying around the edges, threatening to unravel and leave her adrift in a sea of hopelessness. How much more could she take? The murder of Father Benedicto, their abduction and imprisonment, Jack Spurgeon's crucifixion, the constant threats, the sexual violence just now committed against Dianne... it all coalesced into a cold, black lump of despair that made it difficult to feel God's presence.

Is this where it ends? she wondered. *Is this where my faith is destroyed once and for all?*

Engulfed by the darkness, it really felt that way.

Not knowing what else to do, she bowed her head and prayed. *Lord, I'm begging you, give me a sign, give me something, anything, to hold onto. Let me know that You're still there, that You haven't broken Your promise to never leave me or forsake me. Give me the strength to not falter in the faith. Because honestly, Lord, I feel like I'm about to lose it.*

The answer did not come immediately, but in her experience, answers to prayer rarely did. However, as the night dragged on, Amber found herself remembering the apostles and the gruesome torments they had suffered as they spread the gospel throughout the land in the wake of Christ's resurrection.

Peter, crucified upside down.

James, beheaded.

Bartholomew, flayed with knives.

James, stoned to death.

Simon, sawed in half.

These early believers had suffered hate and persecution and torture and, ultimately, excruciating deaths, and not a single one of them ever wavered in their faith. Bound in chains, beaten, clubbed, spat upon, tormented, and finally, executed, they all clung to the hope they had found in Jesus Christ.

Despite the violent, bloody, disturbing images in her mind, Amber nevertheless smiled. *Thanks for the reminder, Lord.*

She steeled herself for whatever came next and vowed it would not break her.

FOURTEEN

STONE SURVEYED HIS SURROUNDINGS, eyes swiveling in their sockets, taking it all in. The busted streetlights, cracked concrete, dilapidated buildings, and rusting warehouses made it clear they were in a bad part of town. A three-legged mongrel dog slunk out of an alley and hobbled away, giving them a look that seemed to say, *What the fuck are you doing here?* It reminded him of Max, probably conked out on the end of the bed at this very moment, snoring away.

It gave Stone a pang of homesickness that he quickly pushed aside. No time for that shit right now. He needed to stay focused, not think about what he had to lose back in Whisper Falls.

Braxx sat beside him in the SUV that Bianca had loaned them, staring out the bug-splattered windshield at the ghetto outside. The only illumination in the area came from a single yellow light hanging above the door of the warehouse they had been directed to. Moths fluttered there, banging their wings against the jaundiced-colored bulb.

"Not the worst shithole I've ever seen," Braxx

muttered. "That being said, there ain't no saints hanging around these parts."

"Saints don't sell black market weapons," said Stone. "Tonight, I'll take the sinners."

"Or get taken by them. I've got a bad feeling about this."

"What we've got is limited options," Stone replied. "Besides, Bianca said it's just this guy Carlito and a four-man goon squad. You telling me we can't handle five assholes?"

Braxx shrugged. "I'd feel better if we were packing heat. Not a big fan of walking into a situation like this with no guns on us."

"Thought your fists and feet were registered as lethal weapons."

"They're not made of Kevlar. Need to make sure we don't get shot before I get close enough to rip out some throats with my bare hands." His fingers curled into claws as if instinctively responding to the thought.

"Let's hope it doesn't come to that," Stone said. "We give them the cash, they give us the guns, and we get the hell out of here. No games, no bullshit, no fucking around."

"You know, you cuss a lot for a preacher."

"So I've been told. Bother you?"

Braxx grinned and winked. "Negative, *padre*. I think it's hot."

"You're such a jackass."

"Now you're just teasing me."

Stone rolled his eyes and reached for the door handle. "Let's get this over with."

As they exited the SUV and approached the ware-house, Stone carried a black duffel bag stuffed with enough cash to purchase what they needed, as long as the price was reasonable. If the gun dealers got greedy, Stone would have to either negotiate with them or settle for less hardware.

He had done deals like this hundreds of times during his warrior days. Sometimes they went smooth and easy, like a well-greased machine. Other times they went sideways and turned into a royal clusterfuck. You just never knew what you were walking into.

The warehouse door opened before they reached it. Moths scattered at the sudden motion but immediately returned and resumed flapping against the piss-yellow bulb. The weak, watery light illuminated a short but hard-muscled Latino man with a red bandanna wrapped around his head, a black leather vest on his otherwise bare torso, and fingerless gloves that exposed knuckles tattooed with spiderwebs. His left hand pushed the door open while the right held a long-barreled, stainless-steel .357 Magnum revolver down by his thigh. The hammer wasn't cocked but his finger tapped against the trigger. His dark eyes peered at Stone and Braxx as the two men drew close. "You the *hombres* our mutual friend told us to expect?"

"We're not with the Jehovah's Witnesses, if that's what you're wondering," Braxx replied.

The man grinned, exposing a gold-capped tooth. "Maybe you are with those Girl Scouts I have heard about in America, here to sell me some Samoa cookies."

Braxx shot Stone a sideways glance. "Samoas? I can't do business with somebody that likes Samoas. Everybody knows the Thin Mints are where it's at."

Stone ignored him and said, "Listen, pal, we're not here to sell shit. We're here to buy shit. Can we get on with it?"

The Mexican made a *tsk-tsk* sound and shook his head in mock sadness. "Americans...so impatient and no sense of humor."

"We can all have a laugh riot once I've got some guns in my hands," Stone replied.

"Fine, let's get down to business then," Gold Tooth said, nodding his head toward the interior of the warehouse. "Right this way."

Stone and Braxx stepped through the open door, brushing past Gold Tooth. Neither of them liked having an armed man at their back but it couldn't be helped. Stone noticed Braxx keeping his head slightly turned, maintaining view of the guy at their six with his peripheral vision. If that revolver came up, Braxx would pounce on Gold Tooth like a wolf pouncing on a rabbit, and the results would be pretty much the same—blood and carnage.

The interior of the warehouse was pretty much wall-to-wall vehicles, some of them intact, most of them in various stages of dismantlement. Tires were stacked in haphazard columns or thrown into piles. Three engine blocks dangled from chains. A heap of fenders nestled in a corner next to a workbench full of metal saws, torches, sockets, and oily rags. It looked like someone had set off a bomb in there and sent car and truck parts flying in all directions.

Four men, all Latinos, leaned against a Chevy Silverado sitting on cinderblocks, the windshield missing, and the cargo box stripped down to the chassis. A folding table in front of them was loaded with weaponry and ammo and stacks of magazines preloaded with cartridges. Like Gold Tooth bringing up the rear behind them, all the men wore red bandannas wrapped around their heads like it was some kind of uniform.

Stone didn't give a damn about how they dressed. He did give a damn that they all sported hardware—holstered, at least for now, except for the guy behind them—while he and Braxx remained unarmed. Hopefully he would change that in the next few minutes.

He raked his gaze over the quartet. "I'm supposed to ask for Carlito."

One of the men, sporting a goatee and little green tears tattooed at the corners of his eyes, pushed away from the Chevy, rolled his shoulders, and stood up straight. "I am Carlito. Bianca vouched for you. *Bienvenido.*"

"Nice chop shop you got going here," Stone said.

Carlito shrugged. "It pays the bills."

"So, you boost cars and sell guns. Anything else I need to know?"

"Suffice it to say that I am an *hombre* of many talents, and you know what you need to know." He gestured at the table in front of him, waving his hand over the pistols, carbines, submachine guns, grenades, magazines, and ammunition like a show host displaying the grand prize. "As you can see, I have obtained everything you requested, and on *mucho* short notice. Two HK UMP-45s, two HK416 carbines, two Glock 21s, frag grenades as well as flashbangs, and magazines and ammo for all of them."

"What, no surface to air missiles?" Braxx grunted. "What kind of gun dealer are you?"

Carlito ignored him, his attention focused on Stone. "I trust it looks *bueno* to you?"

"Looks fine." Stone tossed the satchel of money. It landed with a heavy thud on the concrete floor next to the table. "Not sure how much Bianca told you, but we've got a ticking clock situation, so I'm not interested in wasting time with a bunch of back-and-forth bullshit. What's in that bag is more than a fair price for everything on the table. You take the money, we'll take the hardware, and let's be done with this."

One of the other goons grabbed the satchel, unzipped

it, and quickly counted the cash. He zipped it back up and gave Carlito a nod.

The gun dealer smirked at Stone. "That all sounds *excelente*, except for one small change."

"And what would that be?" Stone asked, but he already had a strong suspicion.

"Dammit," Braxx muttered. "I fucking knew it."

"We'll take the money," Carlito said, "but you're not taking the hardware." His smirk broadened into a full-fledged smile, cold and mirthless. "And I'm not interested in any back-and-forth bullshit *negociaciones* either. You can accept your losses and walk out of here alive, or we can just kill you and toss your bodies in a car crusher." He shrugged. "Doesn't matter much to me either way, *cabron*."

"Great," Braxx growled. "A fucking double cross. I told you I had a bad feeling about these bastards."

"You been paying attention?" Stone asked.

"Of course," Braxx replied. "Amateur hour up in this bitch."

Carlito scowled. "What are you two *hijos de puta* talking about?"

"Your mistake," Stone said. "Not your only one, but your biggest one."

The scowl deepened. "Mistake? What mistake?"

"Only one of you has their gun out."

Braxx exploded into motion so fast that Stone couldn't even really tell what he did. One minute he was just standing there looking all pissed off; the next he was a tornado of violent action, a spinning, whirling, punching, kicking dervish of destruction. In something close to a nanosecond, he had disarmed Gold Tooth behind them, had the long-barreled revolver in his hand, and was using the man's body as a human shield. Carlito and the other three foot-soldiers had barely begun to draw their guns.

Stone wasn't as fast as Braxx, but he was plenty fast enough to dive forward and kick the leg of the table so that the table tipped toward him, spilling its lethal contents. He snatched an UMP-45 practically out of midair with one hand and snatched up a magazine full of .45 caliber man-killers with the other.

As he slapped the magazine home, he heard the .357 Magnum in Braxx's grasp buck and boom, sending a peal of thunder through the warehouse. As he powered up into a combat crouch, he saw the gun dealer to Carlito's right flopping to the ground with a gaping hole punched through his chest, left of center, the big-bore bullet blowing apart his heart.

By then, Carlito and the other two men had managed to drag their pistols into play.

Stone triggered a quick burst from the HK submachine gun that tore into another guy's lower abdomen and folded him in half. As Stone rolled across the concrete floor to seek concealment under a car that hadn't been chopped to scrap yet, he heard the foot-soldier howling in pain. Getting gut shot did that to a man. Nothing worse than having your intestines scrambled by sizzling-hot hollow-points. Stone had heard it described as having a buzzsaw rip through your bowels.

Carlito's attention was focused on Braxx, who was busy dragging Gold Tooth toward a pile of tires that he could use for cover and concealment. Braxx's short stature served him well in this situation, as he was able to easily hide behind his much taller human shield. The 9mm automatic in the gun dealer's fist spat flame and lead and showed zero loyalty toward Gold Tooth, who took the hits like the involuntary barrier Braxx had intended. Blood spurted in hot red jets from his torso as his body shuddered spastically from the hammering impacts.

Braxx grunted as one of the bullets punched through Gold Tooth's shoulder and gouged a raw trench in the meat of his upper arm. He shoved the bullet-riddled body/shield away and hunkered down behind the small mountain of tires. The pile of rubber was plenty thick enough to absorb any slugs that came his way. But he knew he couldn't stay here long. Carlito or the other remaining henchman would try to circle around behind him.

He took a quick glance at the injury. Nothing more than a deep flesh wound. Certainly nothing that would keep him out of the fight and the blood streaming down his arm barely even registered. Lord knew he had suffered a whole lot worse than this scratch.

Concealed beneath the car, Stone saw Gold Tooth's shot-to-hell body hit the ground like a slab of dead meat. That meant just Carlito and one other gun dealer remained standing. The gut shot goon continued to howl his agony for the world to hear but appeared to be very much out of commission. Less than ten seconds had passed since Braxx made his move and the odds had narrowed considerably.

Carlito broke left, keeping junked vehicles between him and Braxx's position, trying to circle around for a shot, as expected. The other guy rolled to the right, closing in on Stone's position, trying to catch a glimpse and get him in his gunsights.

But just because he couldn't see Stone did not mean Stone couldn't see him. From underneath the car, the man's body might not be visible but his ankles sure were. Stone hit the UMP's trigger and sent a swarm of .45 caliber bullets out between the car's two front tires that pretty much amputated the guy's feet. Flesh, bone, blood, and tendons flew apart and the target crumpled to the concrete, shrieking even louder than his gut shot partner. Stone slammed a follow-up salvo into the bastard's head and silenced him with brain-bursting kill-shots that sent skull chunks skittering across the floor.

"You cocksuckers!" Carlito shouted. "You have no idea who you're messing with!"

You should have just taken the money and walked away, dipshit, Stone thought.

He scrambled out from under the car and powered to his feet, scanning the warehouse for Carlito. Where the hell was he? Then he spotted the gun dealer's bandanna wrapped head moving just above the door frame of a partially disassembled Buick sedan. But when Stone raised the UMP-45 to draw a bead on the in motion target, Carlito ducked down out of sight.

Shit.

Stone started moving to his left, trying to get a better angle.

Carlito bellowed, "I got something for you, *pendajo!*"

His arm came into view just long enough to lob a grenade toward Braxx's position behind the tires.

"Braxx!" Stone yelled. "Grenade!"

He glimpsed Braxx bolting from cover and diving into the cargo bed of a nearby pickup truck. The grenade completed its arc and exploded. The razored shrapnel slashed through the tires and sent rags of rubber flying everywhere. Stone kept the UMP raised and ready, waiting for Carlito to show himself.

Come on, you son of a bitch. Let's get this over with.

As if Stone's wish was the gun dealer's command, Carlito popped up with his pistol blazing. At least one of the shots came damn close to getting lucky, scorching past Stone's ear close enough for him to feel the heat of its passing. He flinched his head to the side and lost the fraction of a second he needed to get Carlito bracketed in his gunsights.

Braxx didn't have that problem.

He rose from the bed of the truck with snake-strike speed, firing the .357 Magnum revolver while still in motion. The gun-blast sounded like a dragon's roar reverberating off the corrugated metal walls of the warehouse. The heavy slug smashed into Carlito's left shoulder socket and blew apart the joint in an eruption of torn flesh and shattered bone. It didn't quite take his arm off, but it was damn close, hanging on by just a few mangled strings of meat and muscle.

The impact spun the gun dealer around as if he'd been walloped by a wrecking ball. Stone hit the trigger and blasted a half-dozen .45 caliber projectiles into Carlito's neck and face, ending the firefight in a gruesome explosion of gore. The body hit the ground, twitched its way through a series of death spasms, and then was still.

Stone walked over to make sure the man was dead. Not that a bunch of bullets to the kisser left room for much doubt, but stranger things had happened. Braxx joined him, staring down at the bloody corpse. "Well, that went well," he said.

"He got greedy and he got dead," Stone replied. He saw the blood streaming down his friend's arm. "You're bleeding."

Braxx grinned and lowered his voice to an extra-macho growl like some kind of '80s action hero. "I ain't got time to bleed."

Stone shook his head. "You watch too many movies, man."

"Hey, that's a classic."

A long, drawn-out groan came from near the overturned table.

"You leave one still breathing?" Braxx asked.

"Put some lead in his guts. Didn't have time to finish him off."

"Gut shot?" Braxx made a disappointed clucking sound with his tongue. "I thought you were some kind of badass slinger, all about the headshots."

"Says the hypocrite who shot the last guy in the shoulder."

"Hey, that's all I could see from my angle. Have to take the shot you're given, not wait for the one you want. You wait for that perfect shot, you might find yourself getting your ass zapped."

They walked over to the gut shot gun dealer writhing on the ground in a widening pool of blood and gastric juices. His red bandanna had come off somewhere along the way, revealing a shaved skull tattooed with horned devils, sexy nuns, and various incarnations of "666." He stared up at them in misery. "*Por favor*, call an ambulance."

"You don't need an ambulance," Stone said, leveling the submachine gun. "You need a coroner." He took the top of the guy's head off with a short burst.

Braxx stared down at the twitching corpse. "No mercy, huh?"

"I thought about dragging him under one of those engine blocks and dropping it on his head. Compared to that, a couple bullets in the head might be considered merciful." He gave Braxx a look. "Why, you got a problem with it?"

Braxx shook his head. "Nah, just surprised, is all. Thought you became a preacher because you were sick of all the killing."

"It's complicated," Stone replied.

"Not really. The son of a bitch got what he deserved. Simple as that." Braxx spat on the corpse.

They gathered up the weapons, reclaimed the satchel

full of money—the dead men didn't need the cash—and headed back to the SUV. In this part of town at this time of night, it was unlikely anybody would call the police over some gunshots, even if anyone was around the warehouse district to hear them. Somebody would discover the bodies eventually—or, hell, maybe the rats would take care of them—but by then, Stone and Braxx would be long gone, preferably back over the border with their mission successfully completed.

They secured the hardware and cash in the back of the SUV and then climbed into the cab. As Stone pushed the button to start the vehicle and the engine rumbled to life, Braxx said, "You know it's entirely possible that Bianca stuck it to us and orchestrated this double cross."

Stone shifted into gear and swung the SUV through a tight U-turn to face back the way they had come. As he punched the gas, headlights piercing the night, he growled, "That's what we're going to find out, and God help her if it's true."

FIFTEEN

THEY WOUND their way through the streets back to Bianca's safehouse without incident, occasionally doubling back and making random turns in case they were being tailed from the warehouse. Simple, basic evasive maneuvers that proved unnecessary, but neither of them had survived this long by taking chances.

Stone tried to tamp down the anger he felt. He knew he shouldn't jump to conclusions. Black market gun brokers were a notoriously sketchy bunch, and this was hardly the first time someone had tried to burn him during a weapons acquisition. The fact that these clowns, recommended by Bianca, had tried to kill them did not automatically mean that she had orchestrated the betrayal.

Still, Stone intended to get some answers.

Once they were inside, Bianca took one look at them, shook her head, and said, "I guess things didn't go well, huh?"

"What's the matter?" said Stone. "Sorry to see us still breathing?"

Bianca's eyes narrowed. "And exactly what the hell is that supposed to mean?"

Stone ignored the question. "Braxx caught some lead. Can you patch him up?"

"It's a goddamned graze," Braxx grunted. "Will you fucking relax already?"

Bianca walked over and examined the wound. "Looks like it missed the bone, but not by much. Pretty deep. Needs a couple of stitches."

"Seriously? I've had shaving cuts worse than this," Braxx protested. "Give me a break."

"Got it," Bianca replied. "You're a big, macho tough guy who shaves his *cojones* with a rusty butter knife. But your arm still needs stitches." She headed toward the bathroom. "Follow me and let's get that thing closed up before you get an infection."

Braxx looked at Stone and blinked. "For the record, she's full of shit. The butter knife isn't rusty."

"Great," Stone said. "I may never get that image out of my head."

When he checked on them a few minutes later, Braxx was perched on the edge of the bathtub while Bianca hovered over him, sewing up the ugly-looking trench the bullet had plowed through his arm, working deftly with needle and thread. A first aid kit was open on the bathroom sink within easy reach. Stone spotted a tube of antibiotic ointment and figured Bianca had applied it to the wound before she started stitching. Braxx winced as the needle jabbed in and out of his flesh, pulling the edges tight together and closing things up.

"God, you're such a baby," Bianca said.

"Yeah, well, you're not exactly being gentle," Braxx retorted. "Feels like you're using a railroad spike and barbed wire to patch me up."

"Shut up or I'll rub some salt in there before I finish closing."

"Now you're just teasing me with a good time."

She shook her head. "You're incorrigible."

"I don't know what that means," Braxx said, "but you're probably right."

Stone folded his arms across his chest and stood in the doorway, leaning against the frame, staying quiet until Bianca had finished the stitch job and applied a bandage. As she put away the supplies, he said, "Your guys tried to pull a double cross."

She shrugged. "They're not 'my guys,' Lucas. They're black market gun dealers. It happens. You've been in the game—or were in the game—long enough to know that."

"Or maybe you set us up, told them to take us out, offered them a nice payout for our heads on a platter."

Bianca stiffened at the accusation and her head whipped around to stare at him, eyes flashing wildfire. "And exactly why would I do that?"

"You made it pretty clear earlier that you're angry with me for breaking things off with you. Maybe having your asshole gun runners drop the hammer on us was your way of getting revenge."

Bianca slammed the medicine cabinet door shut a little harder than necessary, rattling the glass in the stainless-steel frame. Then she sighed and shook her head and when she spoke again, it wasn't anger in her voice, but something very close to scorn. "You need to check your ego, Lucas. Your dick isn't so *excelente* that I'm willing to have you murdered just because I can't have it."

"The lady's got a point," Braxx said, rolling down his shirt sleeve to cover the bandaged stitches. "By all accounts, it's really not that impressive."

Stone ignored the cheap shot and kept his eyes locked on Bianca. "You have to admit that it looks kind of strange that right after I turn you down, you send us to some assholes who try to kill us."

"Sorry, but I can't help what it looks like," Bianca replied with a touch of exasperation. "You needed guns quickly, I did the best I could on short notice, the *bastardos* got greedy and tried to have their cake and eat it too. Like I said, it happens, and you damn well know it."

"I'm not convinced," Stone said. "Hell hath no fury like a woman scorned and all that shit."

"Well, maybe this will help." Bianca turned so her whole body faced him and crossed her arms, mimicking his stance. "While you boys were gone, I worked my contacts. Not only do I know *who* took your missionaries, I know *where* they are being held. Plus, I even know how to get you inside."

"I'm listening."

"What, you think I should just hand over the *información* you want and forget that you just insulted me by claiming I tried to have you killed?"

Still sitting on the edge of the tub, Braxx said, "Bianca, we really need that info."

"I know you do, *compinche*. Doesn't change the fact that I've been insulted in my own home."

Stone almost pointed out that this was a safehouse, not her home, but thought better of it. He had already angered her enough. Instead, he said, "An apology, that what you want?"

"You don't think you owe me one after the bullshit you just spouted?"

"I probably do. Sorry."

"That's the best you can do? *Patético.* I've heard more sincerity from a barking dog."

"Are you kidding me?" Stone glanced at Braxx. "You want to help me out here?"

Braxx shrugged. "I dunno, I've heard some pretty

sincere dog barks in my time and that wasn't one of them."

"Thanks, buddy." Stone looked back at Bianca. He captured her eyes with his, tried to draw her in so she would hear the truth in his words as he said, "Bianca, I'm sorry. Things went sideways, we almost got killed, Braxx took a hit, and I let my emotions cloud my better judgment. I apologize for what I said about you being behind it."

She studied his face for a few moments, no doubt searching for the sincerity she sought from him, and then the corner of her mouth tugged up in a playful smile. "I think that would sound better on your knees."

"Well, ain't that wonderful," Braxx muttered. "First you can't even bark as good as a damn dog, now you have to beg like one."

Stone shook his head. "That is absolutely not happening," he said firmly. "I'm afraid of what you would try to have me do while I was down there."

"Probably make you recite some poetry," Braxx said. "She's heard what a cunning linguist you are."

Bianca laughed wickedly and left the bathroom, patting Stone on the chest as she brushed past him. "I'll get you boys a drink, tell you what I found out, and then you can get the hell out of my life."

———

Ten minutes later, they were all sitting in the living room with drinks in hand—a can of Coke for Stone, bottled water for Braxx, and a glass of white wine for Bianca—and Stone felt himself growing impatient. He was restless, his nerves on edge. He needed to be on the move, engaging in some sort of action to rescue the missionaries, not sitting here sipping soda like it was some kind of social hour. But he resisted expressing his impatience, knowing Bianca would just drag things out even longer, taking some kind of perverse, petty pleasure in torturing him. She had proven more than once that she could be a vindictive woman.

No, he would sit here and drink his Coke, and she would tell them when she was damn well ready.

Thank God, she didn't drag it out too long.

"The missionaries were taken by a mid-level member of the Juarez cartel named Armando Ochoa," she said once she had sipped her wine down to the halfway mark and then refilled the glass. "He is also known as *El Crucificador*."

"The Crucifier," Stone said. "That makes sense, given the video he sent to Father Andy."

"Sounds like a professional wrestling name," Braxx grunted.

"Long story short," Bianca continued, "Ochoa has a serious vendetta against the church."

"St. Luke's?"

She shook her head. "Not a specific church. The church as a whole, as an organization, as an entity. He was abused as a boy and now harbors a grudge. A indulges this grudge by kidnapping missionaries, crucifying some of them as an example or vengeance or whatever, and then ransoms the rest."

Stone tried not to think about how Andy would have reacted if Amber had ended up crucified. And the threat still remained. As long as she and the other missionaries were in Ochoa's clutches, they were in danger of the nails. It was a horror he didn't even want to consider right now.

Bianca quickly filled them in on all the details, or at least the ones she knew. Stone and Braxx listened intently, filing away the information, mentally sifting through it, analyzing it, looking for ways it could be used to accomplish their mission.

"Okay," Stone said when Bianca wrapped up her intelligence report. "You said they're being held on a compound that's also a farm."

"Used to be horses there, but from what I'm being told, it's primarily pigs now," Bianca said. "But yes, it's basically a hobby farm. The cartel uses the barns to store narcotics, and the pigs are used for body disposal."

"And you know a way for us to get inside?"

Bianca smiled. "You catch a ride with the pigs."

She explained the plan.

Braxx looked impressed. "That actually works."

"If everything goes right," Bianca said, "then yes, it will work just fine."

"How reliable is your intel?" Stone asked.

"No guarantees, but generally solid," Bianca replied. "That being said, I didn't have a lot of time to work, so none of this has been verified."

"So our heads could be on the chopping block again."

Bianca shrugged. "That's the risk you take in this business."

Stone looked over at Braxx. "It's not just my risk. You get a say in this too."

Braxx snorted. "If I said I was sitting this one out, you'd just go without me."

"That's true."

"I owe you my life, man. I'm not gonna leave your butt swinging bare ass in the breeze with no one to watch it."

"You really could have worded that better," Stone said. "But thanks."

"Don't mention it."

Bianca drained the rest of her wine in one gulp, set the glass down on the coffee table, and stood up. "Well, good luck, boys. You've got a four-hour drive ahead of you, so you better get going."

"Right." Stone set down his Coke can and stood up. "Thanks for everything, Bianca. You really came through for us. If you ever need something—"

Before he could finish the sentence, she was right in front of him, close enough that you couldn't have passed a pencil between their bodies. "You can take the 'I owe you one' speech and shove it up your *culo*," she said. "I never want to see you again, Lucas Stone."

"Bianca, I—"

She shushed him with a hard, passionate, almost violent kiss. Stone started to pull away, but she kissed him even harder, practically crushing his lips with hers. He could feel the hurt, taste the pain, sense the heartache, and something in the way she trembled let him know this truly was goodbye forever. He let it happen, not really responding, not wanting to give her any hope, but no longer pulling away. He let her have what she needed for closure, nothing more.

She finally broke the kiss, chest heaving slightly, face flushed with all sorts of emotions, and whispered, "Thank you." Then she pointed to the door. "Now get the fuck out of my life and never come back."

SIXTEEN

SIX HOURS LATER, Stone and Braxx were concealed in a cluster of boulders and creosote brush on top of a small hill overlooking the hard-packed road that threaded through the desert landscape toward the compound of Armando Ochoa, approximately five miles away. The newly risen sun was starting to heat things up but not to an unbearable degree.

Besides, if things went according to plan, they wouldn't be laying here long enough to get scorched and baked.

"You think this will actually work?" Braxx asked.

"You seemed all for it when Bianca mentioned it," Stone said.

"That was a long time ago."

"Six hours is a long time?"

"Long enough for me to realize that the plan is solid but not exactly foolproof."

"You got a better idea?" Stone watched a whip scorpion scuttle over the arid ground nearby, looking significantly more ferocious than it actually was. It gave him an idea for a sermon about how hard, hostile exteriors were often just a defense mechanism to shield the soft heart within.

"No, nothing better comes to mind," Braxx replied. "But I'll *feel* a whole lot better when this fucking truck actually shows up and I know this plan might actually have a shot."

Three minutes later, Stone said, "I think you can start feeling better." He pointed in the distance where an approaching vehicle was raising a dust cloud into the dawn air. With no breeze to break it down, it just hung there like a dirty cloak above the road.

"About goddamned time," Braxx grumbled. "I hate sitting around playing twiddle-dick, waiting for something to happen."

"Patience was never one of your virtues."

"Nope." Braxx grinned. "Always had to get by on my devastatingly good looks, unmatched sexual prowess, and superb ass-kicking abilities."

"One out of three ain't bad," Stone said.

As the vehicle rumbled closer, continuing to raise a cloud of dust, the two warriors checked their weapons. For what they had planned, they opted for HK416 carbines, each one loaded with a thirty-round magazine packed with 5.56mm cartridges. They hoped to pull off this next phase of the rescue mission without firing a single shot, but just in case things didn't go according to plan, both HKs sported sound suppressors. It was unlikely that anyone at the compound five miles away would have heard a shot even without the suppressors, but there was no reason to take the chance.

Glock pistols, also suppressed, hung low in tactical holsters, nylon straps tight around their thighs to secure everything in place and ensure a smooth draw if necessary. The rest of the weapons remained in a duffel bag tucked behind a rock. If they couldn't pull this off with

HKs and Glocks, they didn't deserve to succeed, and they had no desire or intention to turn this place into a warzone.

As the vehicle rounded a bend and started down the straightway that would lead them right to Stone and Braxx's position, they confirmed that it was, indeed, the target vehicle—a white, six-wheeled, flat-nosed truck with a two-tiered livestock delivery cage on the back. The cage was comprised of heavy-gauge steel with narrow slots for the pigs inside to get air.

"Let's get this show on the road," Braxx said, clearly ready for some action.

Stone gave him no argument. The time had come to move.

The whip scorpion darted away as the two men rose from their prone positions and quickly made their way down the hill, dirt and stones tumbling down the slope in front of them. They weren't trying to be stealthy or hidden. They reached the bottom, stood in the center of the road, and aimed their rifles at the dust-coated windshield as the truck slowed down in a harsh grinding of gears and shuddered to a halt. Through the glass, Stone saw two Latino men, both with their hands raised at shoulder level in the universal sign of surrender.

Stone circled to the driver's side while Braxx went the other way, keeping his sights on the passenger. Neither of them had any intention of pulling the trigger; as far as they knew, the truck's occupants were innocent. Unless things devolved into a self-defense situation, Stone and Braxx planned to gain compliance through threat of violence rather than actual violence.

Stone pointed the muzzle of the HK at the driver. "Get out," he commanded, hoping the guy understood him. "Rápidamente."

The man nodded and slowly lowered his left hand to

reach for the door handle. Stone kept a careful eye on him, watching for any sudden movements that would signal a threat. He didn't want to kill this guy but would not hesitate to light him up if a gun appeared.

But nothing happened other than the door swinging open with the creaking protest of rusty hinges. The driver climbed down from behind the wheel and stood facing Stone, both hands back up in the air. He appeared to be in his late thirties, maybe early forties, with nondescript features. He was dressed in loose-fitting clothes stained with dark smudges that was presumably either dirt or pig manure.

Braxx repeated the process with the passenger—younger but dressed similarly—and then herded him around to the other side to stand next to his partner. Both men looked terrified, sweat that had nothing to do with the rising sun streaming down their nervous faces.

"Either one of you speak English?" Stone asked. Having determined these guys were not a threat, Stone kept the muzzle of his carbine lowered so it aimed at their feet rather than center mass.

The driver nodded. "*Si, senor.* I do, but Diego—" He canted his head to the side to indicate the passenger. "—he does not."

"Then I'll tell you what's about to happen and you can translate after."

The driver nodded again and said, "*Si.*"

"What's your name?" Stone asked.

"I am Hector, *senor.*"

Pink pig nostrils were sticking out through the ventilation slots in the livestock cage, snorting and snuffing and trying to figure out why the truck had stopped moving. Stone knew that, contrary to popular myth, pigs actually didn't smell bad. Their dung, however, was a different matter, and the pungent scent wafted into his nostrils.

"The hogs," Stone said. "You're delivering them to Armando Ochoa, right?"

"*Si, senor.* We bring him a fresh batch of *cerdos* and take the old ones out for slaughter. When it is done, we bring him back the meat."

"So, he's expecting you?"

"*Si.* Yes." Hector nodded. "We are expected and will be missed if we do not show up."

"Don't worry, you're going to show up," Stone said. He raised the HK416 and canted it over his shoulder, removing the immediate threat from the equation. "We're coming with you."

Hector gestured at the truck's small cab. "*Perdóneme*, but there is not enough room for all of us, *senor*. We cannot all fit."

"Diego will stay here. You can pick him up later. I'll take his place upfront. My friend here—" Stone cocked his head toward Braxx. "—will ride in the back."

"*En la parte de atrás?* With the pigs?"

Stone nodded.

"Can't fucking wait," Braxx grumbled. "Gonna be wallowing in pig shit like the prodigal son."

Hector looked perplexed. "*Señor*, do you...do you know who Armando Ochoa is?"

"I know enough," Stone replied. "I know he took something that doesn't belong to him, and I want it back."

"*Senor* Ochoa, he is a bad man. He *muy malvado*, very evil."

"Tell me something I don't know," Stone said. "When I'm done with the son of a bitch, he'll be shaking hands with *el diablo*."

"Maybe I could just stay here with Diego?" Hector

suggested hopefully. "You and your friend take the truck and do what you have to do."

"Sorry," Stone said, "but that won't cut it. I'm sure there are guards at the entrance, and they need to see a familiar face when we roll up."

Hector hung his head and looked miserable. "You are bringing me to my death, *señor*."

"Oh, I'm bringing death all right," Stone rasped. "But not to you."

As Hector translated everything to Diego, Stone reflected on the fact that he was fully immersed in his warrior persona once again, putting it on like a welcome set of old clothes. Or maybe more like a cobra trying to get back into the dead skin it had shed. The preacher side of him, the man he had become when he walked away from the black ops killing fields, seemed a million miles away at the moment.

You're trusting your guns more than God right now, an inner voice warned.

Stone knew the voice wasn't wrong, but he also knew that right now was not the time to dwell on the matter. Seeking justification, fretting about finding the balance between his preacher side and his warrior side, worrying about the spectrum between good and evil and where he fell on it...all that mental noise would do right now was distract him and quite possibly get him killed. He had to put it out of his mind like unwanted emotional detritus and not think about it, lock it away in the same mental compartment he had tucked Holly and Lizzy into until this mission was over. Time enough for reflection when—if—they got back home.

He glanced over and caught Braxx staring at him with narrowed—and worried—eyes, looking like he could read Stone's mind and see the troubled thoughts. And hell, given the bond they shared, maybe he could.

"You all right, man?" Braxx asked. "Looking lost there for a second."

Stone nodded. "Just got some things to figure out when this over."

"Like how to make your preacher side and warrior side coexist?" Braxx asked, proving Stone's mind-reading suspicions.

Stone nodded again.

"You know," Braxx said, "you might have to accept the fact that maybe they never will. Maybe it's like trying to make a peanut butter and jelly sandwich when all you've got to work with is peanut butter and mayonnaise."

"And how do I live with that?"

"Hell if I know." Braxx shrugged. "I guess maybe you just do."

Hector finished explaining everything to Diego. They left the man with some bottled water they had carried with them in the weapons satchel and had Hector assure him they would pick him up on the way back. Diego looked skeptical, but it wasn't like he really had a choice.

Braxx took the weapon satchel and climbed into the back with the pigs, who seemed pretty nonplussed about having a human join them, welcoming him with curious grunts and nudging him with pink noses. He crawled up to the corner directly behind the passenger seat and got as comfortable as possible, his clothes smeared with swine dung.

"Damn it, Luke," he grumbled. "When I said I'd go through some shit with you, I didn't mean it literally."

"You got a better plan?"

"Yeah, you get back here with the goddamned hogs, and I ride up front all nice and comfy."

"Too late now," Stone said. "You'd get pig shit all over the seat."

Braxx kicked at a hog trying to gnaw on his boot. It retreated with an indignant squeal. "I need new friends."

Hector climbed back up behind the steering wheel, and Stone settled in next to him to ride shotgun. He had swapped the HK carbine for a pistol, which he kept in his hand. Not aimed directly at Hector, but still pointed in his general direction. "You understand what we're doing?" Stone asked.

"*Si, señor*, I understand."

"Am I going to have any trouble from you?"

"No, *señor*."

Stone held up Glock. "I'm going to put my pistol away. Don't try anything stupid and make me take it back out. We clear?"

"*Si, señor*."

"Good." Stone shoved the handgun back into its holster and gestured at the road ahead, the dirt looking hot and dusty in the morning sun. "Let's go."

SEVENTEEN

TWO THOUSAND MILES AWAY, Holly had her back to the door of the Birch Bark Diner. She had drawn the early shift today and had just flicked the switch to light up the red neon "Open" sign in the window that faced State Route 3. Another waitress would arrive in a couple hours to help with the pre-workday breakfast rush, but right now it was just Holly and the cook to handle the few early risers who would straggle in, as well as the group of elderly gentlemen who showed up religiously to drink coffee, eat homemade pie, and argue politics. Sometimes they got bored with that topic and switched to religion. She had even overheard them talking about Stone and his unorthodox approach to faith a time or two. Most seemed to appreciate his style, but a couple of the old-timers felt that church traditions should be followed.

When her alarm clock went off this morning—Lizzy teased her about using an actual clock, insisting that only old people did that—she had slapped it into silence and then immediately reached for her phone, hoping to see a text from Stone. But there was nothing. He had not even opened the good night text she had sent before going to sleep. She had suppressed the initial surge of disappointment and reminded herself that he was on a dangerous mission, not lollygagging around some resort on vacation.

She tried not to think about the fact that his lack of response could mean he was in trouble, or even dead. She told herself that he was fine, he was busy doing what needed to be done, and he would be home soon. Thinking about any other outcome made her heart hurt.

The bell above the diner door jingled, announcing the first customer of the day. Holly welcomed the sound. Having something to do would take her mind off Stone.

She put a welcoming smile on her face and turned around with a friendly greeting on her lips.

The smile wilted, and the greeting died stillborn when she saw Deacon David White standing there. They were replaced with a teeth-baring snarl and a hissed, "What the hell are you doing here?"

White seemed genuinely taken aback by her hostility. "Um, breakfast?" he said cautiously, slowly, dragging out each syllable as if he was afraid speaking quickly would set her off even more.

"You've got some kind of nerve, coming in here after what you did last night."

White furrowed his brow. "What on earth are you talking about, Holly? I stopped by your house for a visit, you asked me to leave, and I complied. Despite our disagreement regarding our future together, nothing that happened last night would seem to merit the kind of anger you're directing at me right now."

"Did you conveniently forget about the text you sent after you left?"

"Text? I have no idea what you're talking about. What text?"

"The *filthy* one, you perverted son of a bitch." Holly plucked her phone from her back pocket, pulled up the message, and started reading it out loud, enunciating the worst parts for emphasis.

She only made it through four sentences before White, blushing like a nun at an orgy, held up his hand. "Please, stop," he said. "I've heard more than enough."

"What are you turning all red for?" Holly snapped. "You're the one who wrote this crap."

"I most certainly did not, I assure you. Not that you believe me, but I would never disrespect you like that. I would never disrespect *any* woman like that, for that matter. I'm a man of God, a righteous man, and I do everything in my power to live a clean, holy life."

"I guess you need to try harder because there's nothing clean or holy or righteous or godly about the garbage you sent me."

"How many times do I have to tell you? I didn't send that text!" White protested.

"Yeah, right," Holly scoffed. "I tell you I'm not interested in your creepy advances, send you packing, and just minutes later I get this nasty text, and I'm supposed to believe it's not you? Come on, David, I'm not that stupid."

White sighed and seemed to resign himself to her anger. "I can see there is no point in arguing with you, because your mind is clearly made up. You're wrong, but you're free to believe whatever you like."

"Thanks for your permission," Holly said dryly. "What I believe is that if you send me any more texts like that—or any texts at all, for that matter—I'm going to knock your teeth down your throat."

White shook his head. "You can tell you've been hanging around Stone too much. You're starting to sound like him and becoming more and more violent."

"Starting?" Holly put her hands on the counter and leaned forward aggressively. The silver cross around her neck—the one that concealed a small dagger—swung freely, bouncing against her breastbone. Her blouse scooped a little lower than usual since her regular polo shirt was stuffed in the laundry basket, so she had no doubt that she was giving White an eyeful of decent cleavage, but she didn't give a damn. "I shot that survivalist a couple years ago when he came to our house to murder us, and I killed the drug-dealing bitch who burned my daughter's friend alive and dared to try to take Lizzy away from me. When I say I've got a body count, I'm not talking about sexual partners, I'm talking about people I've put six feet under. So don't stand there and act like today is the first time I've ever been violent."

White looked mighty pleased with himself as if he had just won some sort of argument. Holly wanted to grab a frying pan and wipe the smug expression off his face. "Exactly," the head deacon said. "And none of those things happened until Lucas Stone rolled into town in that ancient relic he calls a truck. He shows up and boom, next thing you know, there's killing everywhere and you've got blood on your hands."

"It's not innocent blood, you know. Every person I killed had it coming."

"Blood is blood and because of Stone, you're stained with it."

God, he's such a prick.

Holly pointed at the door. "Get out. Right now, David. Get the hell out of my sight."

"Calm down, I'm going." White took a step back and put his hand on the door handle. "But think about what I said, Holly. Search your heart without it being clouded by whatever affection you have for our cowboy preacher, and you will see that I'm right. Heck, a blind man could see that things were better in Whisper Falls before Stone showed up."

"David, I swear to God, if you don't leave…"

He winked at her—actually *winked* at her, the sanctimonious son of a bitch—and disappeared through the door, the jaunty tinkling of the silver bell announcing his welcomed departure.

Holly watched through the window as White got in his car and drove away, turning right onto Route 3, most likely heading down the road to the church where he spent much of his time fussing about. She felt huge relief when he was no longer in sight. She took several deep breaths to settle her nerves, then resumed setting up for the early morning customers that would show up soon.

While she did not make friends easily—all those years in the Witness Security Program meant she kept most people at arm's length—she did not consider herself to be an unkind person, but she found it extremely hard not to hate David White. His smugly superior and self-righteous style of Christianity had always been off-putting, his advances had always been unwelcomed, and now his raunchy texts had really crossed a line.

As she started wrapping some silverware in napkins, her cell phone vibrated in her back pocket. She took it out and saw she had received a new text from the same unknown number. The same number David White had used to send the pornographic text last night.

This message was shorter but somehow managed to be even more pornographic. The descriptions of what he wanted to do to her were truly disturbing, the sign of a sick, demented mind.

She silently fumed as she shoved the phone back in

her pocket. She hadn't deleted the text from last night and she didn't plan on deleting this one either. They were evidence, proof of harassment. She would show them both to Stone when he got back from Mexico and then sit back with a big old smile on her face while he kicked David White's rotten ass.

EIGHTEEN

AMBER AWOKE to the sound of the stall door being opened and something deep down inside told her that things were about to take a turn for the worse. For as bad as things were, there were always further depths of darkness into which they could plunge.

She had slept fitfully, tucked into the corner of the stall, leaning her head against the wood, trying to ignore the abrasive sting from where the flex cuffs had rubbed her wrists raw and the relentless hunger pains that gnawed at her belly. Since being abducted, the missionaries had been given nothing to eat, only some water. Probably to keep them weak and submissive.

She had been tormented by nightmares of Dianne's screams, cries that seemed to go on forever in the fevered reaches of her mind. Fueled by troubled sleep, her brain conjured up images of what Dianne had suffered in the house and leering, demonic faces and forked-tongue whispers promised her that she would be next. That she would be the next one to return from the house with a dead-eyed gaze, torn clothes, and zombie-like shuffle, broken beyond repair. That the horrors she would suffer at the hands of Armando Ochoa would be too much to bear.

Dianne had remained quiet in her stall for a long time. But eventually she started sobbing uncontrollably, desperate, broken heaves welling up from a fractured soul and a fraying mind. Amber and the others had tried to comfort her, offering hollow platitudes and trite solaces, but they didn't seem to work, and the guards repeated their favorite threat to cut out their tongues if they didn't shut up. Dianne continued sobbing into the dark silence and the guards allowed it, seeming to take some kind of sadistic pleasure from the pain, laughing as they made lewd comments and vocalized their hopes of taking a turn.

Somewhere in the night, Dianne had finally stopped crying, and in the ensuing silence, Amber had finally managed to close her eyes and let exhaustion drift her into an uneasy slumber. The nightmares that haunted her were mostly just memories of the last twelve hours, all the hell they had suffered messing with her mind.

Now she woke up, but the hellish nightmare remained.

A guard stepped into the stall and gestured to her. "Get up." His eyes were cold, his face covered in thick, black stubble.

Amber slowly climbed to her feet. "Where are we going?"

"Shut up or I'll cut your tongue out." The oft-repeated threat seemed automatic at this point. If she had not witnessed Jack being nailed to the cross outside the barn, she would have strongly suspected the threat to be hollow. But she knew these people were evil, capable of horrific cruelty, so severing tongues wasn't out of the question. She had no doubt they had done so in the past and would do so again if that's what it took to achieve compliance from their captives.

The guard shoved her in front of him and prodded her outside. She stumbled a bit, muscles still stiff from being in a sitting position so long and blinked against the rising sun revealing its fire-orange face over the desert hills, promising brutal heat to come once the tolerable warmth of the morning had given way to the furnace-blast rays.

Another guard leaned against the top rail of the pigpen, firing up a cigarette with an electric lighter. He inhaled a lungful of poison and blew it out in a white cloud. It appeared he had just dumped a bucket of slop into the trough and the hogs fought for their food with grunts and squeals, cleft hooves squelching in the thick mud caused by their defecation.

Amber's guard ordered her to halt while he waved at his comrade. "Hey, *amigo*, you got another one of those?"

The guy fished a crumpled pack of smokes from his pocket, shook one out, and offered it to the guard, who accepted with a grateful nod and a contented, *"Gracias, amigo."* He borrowed the lighter and fired up the cigarette, sucking deeply on the nicotine like it was life-giving instead of cancer-causing.

While she stood there and waited for the guard to finish his smoke break, Amber tried her best not to look at the cross towering nearby and the human remains impaled upon it. But her eyes felt compelled to glance in that direction, drawn to the grisly tableau, as if turning away from the horror that had happened would somehow dishonor Jack Spurgeon's tragic death. And dishonor him was the last thing she wanted to do. She needed to look at him and bear witness to what had happened and carry his memory into the future so he would not be forgotten...assuming any of them had a future at all.

She didn't make it three seconds before she had to quickly look away. She just couldn't do it. The coagulated blood from the nail-pierced flesh and his ashen, death-slackened face were bad enough, but the bloated flies crawling on his unblinking eyeballs was more than she could take.

She let out a small gasp as she averted her face and the two guards blew smoke her way and chuckled, dropping insults in Spanish, their tone mocking. She didn't give a single damn. Let them laugh and curse and sneer. She would much rather endure their scorn than ever have to see Jack's tortured corpse again. She tried to block out what she had seen by remembering him in better times, but the bloody images seemed burned on her retinas and forever tattooed on her mind.

Off in the distance, on the remote road that led to the compound, a truck could be seen approaching in a roiling cloud of dust. Even when the truck disappeared behind some hills, the dust cloud rose into the air and marked its forward progress.

"Someone's coming," Amber's guard grunted, stating the obvious. "Are we expecting a shipment today?"

"It's not *narcoticos*," the other guy said. "We're getting a hog delivery today. Old ones out to the butcher, new ones to fatten up." He laughed evilly. "Their first meal will probably be *Señorita* Lillegard's friend hanging up there."

Amber blanched but tried to keep her face blank. She did not want to give them the satisfaction of seeing her disgust and distress. But the thought of Jack being fed to the pigs made her tremble inside. She knew his soul was in a better place, but his mortal remains deserved better than desecration by swine.

Her guard took one last drag on his cigarette, making the tip flare bright orange as he inhaled the last dregs of smoke, and then flicked the butt into the pigpen where it was immediately trampled under the herd of hooves. "Gotta get this *puta* up to *el jefe*," he said. "I'll be back to help you with the hogs while he has his fun."

"*Gracias, mi amigo.*"

"Don't thank me. When I say 'help,' what I really mean is stand around smoking *cigarillos* while I watch you do all the work."

"Same as always, then."

The guard grinned, grabbed Amber by the upper arm, fingers digging in with far more force than necessary, and started hauling her up toward the house. She tried dragging her feet to delay what she knew awaited her there, but it did little good. She was no match for the guard's strength, especially in her exhausted, hungry, weakened condition.

Inside the house, she barely had time to notice all the lavish luxuries adorning the place as she was hauled directly to what turned out to be Ochoa's master suite, a cavernous space that boasted a high, vaulted ceiling and the biggest bed she had ever seen, with crimson sheets and a plethora of pillows.

Ochoa himself stood at the foot of the bed, bracketed by ebony posts carved with skulls, a slight smile on his face. He wore a patterned silk robe that for some reason reminded her of a Navajo blanket, loosely cinched at the waist. She couldn't know for sure, not yet, but she strongly suspected there was nothing underneath the robe.

The guard bowed slightly to his master and retreated, no doubt eager for another cigarette, closing the door behind him. She didn't hear it lock, but the metallic click of the latch engaging had an air of finality that let her know, even with an unlocked door, there was no escaping her fate.

She was alone with the cruelest, most evil man she had ever encountered, and she had little doubt what was about to happen to her. She had no idea why God was choosing to let her suffer this hell, but she prayed for the strength to endure.

As if to confirm her worst fears, Ochoa's smile broadened into something dark and twisted as he said, "I've been looking forward to this moment, *Señorita* Lillegard. Time to break you."

NINETEEN

"WE ARE ALMOST THERE, *SEÑOR*," Hector announced, wrestling with the truck's steering wheel as they bounced over a deep rut. In the back, one of the pigs let out a high-pitched squeal as if protesting the jarring treatment. Stone heard Braxx utter a loud curse but wasn't sure if it was directed at the pig or the pothole.

A moment later they rounded a bend in the road and the main gate of Ochoa's compound came into view up ahead on the right. Hector eased off the gas, slowing the truck's speed. As they approached, Stone saw that the gate itself was constructed of thick metal bars, the hinges buried in thick stone pillars. Maybe they could ram through it if it came down to that, but it wouldn't be easy. The steel barrier looked like it was designed to withstand a tank.

Of course, that made sense. Despite Ochoa's side hustle of kidnapping—and killing—missionaries and raising hogs, the main purpose of this compound and his primary responsibility was storing narcotics for the Juarez cartel. They would have spared no expense in making sure their merchandise was secure.

Stone hoped that their plan for a soft infiltration worked out because if they had to go hard, they might be screwed.

A cluster of small hills with patches of rough, windswept vegetation sprouting from the slopes blocked the gate from the rest of the compound, so whatever happened next, however this infiltration attempt went down, nobody would be able to see them and raise the alarm. Altering the terrain to provide a better tactical view would have been a smarter play on Ochoa's part, but the crucifying cutthroat probably figured nobody would be stupid enough to attack a cartel stronghold.

"Do the guards check the back of the truck?" Stone asked.

Hector gave a little shrug, shifting down into a lower gear. "Not usually, but sometimes. Depends on their mood." He glanced at Stone. "This will be a *problemo, si?*"

"More of a problem for the guy that sticks his face back there," Stone replied, knowing Braxx would be ready with a pistol to deal with any unfortunate search attempts.

Hector shook his head sadly. "I fear there will be *mucho* killing today."

"You're not wrong about that, my friend."

Hector made a scoffing sound in his throat. "If I was your friend, *señor*, you would not have forced me to drive you here at gunpoint."

"Just a figure of speech," Stone said. "And I may have a gun, and you may not be my friend, but I still have no intention of killing you. Play it cool, get us inside that gate, and you're free to go."

"With a bullet in my back."

"With my blessing," Stone replied.

"That's not worth much."

"You're probably right."

They pulled up to the gate and Hector shifted into neutral as two armed men emerged from the guard shack. One held an AK-47 loosely cradled across his chest; the other carried a pistol, but it was snugged into a holster at his side. Clearly, they were not keyed up and on high alert status. Stone realized he could draw and shoot both guards before either one got their weapons into play. Tempting, but he decided to let things play out. He preferred to keep things quiet until the need for violence was absolute. The time for rock 'n' roll would come soon. No need to crank up the volume just yet.

Hector rolled down the driver's side window and greeted both sentries by name. *"Buenos dias,* Fernando. *Buenos dias,* Goyo."

Goyo, the guard with the AK, hung back while Fernando stepped up to the truck. He glanced briefly at Hector and then fastened a suspicious, narrow-eyed stare at Stone. In Spanish, he asked, "Where is Diego?"

"Diego, he is sick," Hector replied without hesitation, the lie rolling easily off his lips. "Puking all night, I am told."

"What happened? He eat something bad?"

Over by the guard shack, Goyo chuckled and said, "Yeah, your momma."

Fernando's face darkened and he spun toward his partner. *"Callate la boca!* Shut your filthy mouth."

Goyo grinned but didn't offer any more off-color commentary.

Fernando turned and faced the truck again, eyes hard as he studied Stone. "So Diego can't make it and the best you can do is replace him with a gringo?"

Hector shrugged. "Beggars cannot be choosers, no? I took what I could get."

"I don't like it," Fernando said. "Change is not good."

Hector shrugged again. "Not bringing the pigs would

not have been good either. *Señor* Ochoa was expecting the shipment today and we did not want to disappoint. If you think it best, we will turn around and come back another day, when Diego is feeling better."

Fernando did not respond, just kept staring at Stone like the gringo was something that had just dropped out of a hog's ass.

In Spanish, Stone asked, "Is there a problem, *amigo?*"

————

In the back of the truck, tucked up in the corner where the livestock carrier met the passenger-side of the cab, Braxx kept several pigs between him and the ventilation slot on the driver's side. Crouched low, smeared with dirt and dung and cloaked in the shadows, with the beasts milling around him, he would be hard to see if the guards merely glanced at the carrier. But a thorough inspection would reveal his presence in about two seconds flat.

It was a little hard to hear over the perpetual grunting of the swine, but Braxx caught enough of the back-and-forth conversation between the guards and the driver to know that things were tense. He held the suppressed Glock 21 in his right hand, a round in the chamber, ready to spit death at a moment's notice. Given what was happening on this cartel compound, the two sentries had little chance of surviving the day no matter what, but they would live a little longer if they let the truck pass through without any trouble.

But it didn't sound like that was the way it was going down.

Braxx touched his finger to the trigger and steeled himself for action.

————

Fernando's eyebrows arched when Stone asked him if there was a problem. He seemed genuinely shocked by the question. His gaze flicked from Stone back to Hector. "Did you not explain the rules to your *companero*? Does he not know that he should not address me unless spoken to?"

Hector squirmed in his seat like something was burning his buttocks. "*Lo siento, señor.* Very, very sorry. He is new and does not understand how things are done."

"He is new, and he looks like trouble, and he is pissing me off," Fernando said. "Enough of this *mierda*." He took three steps back from the truck and gestured at the door. "Out of the fucking truck. Both of you. Right now."

Damn right, enough of this shit, Stone thought. Aloud, he barked, "Braxx! Do it!"

Two *phutt-phutt* sounds came from the back as Braxx fired a suppressed double tap through a ventilation slot and a pair of holes appeared in Fernando's face. One bullet plowed through his left eye and the other impacted on the bridge of his nose, both of them coring through his brain. His head snapped back violently as the contents of his skull burst from the exit wounds and splattered all over Goya.

The other guard flinched and closed his eyes at the sudden spray of bloody muck. Before he could open them, Stone had his Glock out and hit the trigger on his own double tap, sending a pair of bullets across the cab, in front of the driver's face, and out the window where they crashed into Goya's forehead. He toppled to the ground beside Fernando, dead before his body hit the dirt.

Hector sat stiff and rigid in the driver's seat, his face alarmingly pale, his hands on the steering wheel in a white-knuckled grip. He looked scared to move, frozen in place, as if any motion would result in more bullets sizzling past him with just inches to spare. Then, slowly, he reached up and gingerly touched the tip of his nose as if to make sure it was still there and hadn't been shot off.

Stone climbed out of the truck, let Braxx know it was all clear, and stepped over the two fresh corpses to reach the guard shack. He found the gate controller and a moment later the heavy steel bars swung open.

Braxx emerged from the back of the truck covered in sweat and pig shit and cursing up a storm. Even from ten feet away, he smelled ripe and unpleasant. "Next time you call me for help on a fucking mission," he said, "the first question I'll be asking is if there's any chance I'll end up wallowing in shit of any kind. If the answer is yes, you're on your fucking own, my friend."

"Noted," Stone replied. "But I don't know what you're bitching about. We've been in worse places than this before. You forget Syria?"

Braxx immediately sobered. "I'll never forget Syria, man. That's why I'm here."

"You don't owe me anything, G-Man."

"Like hell I don't," Braxx snorted. "Seriously, fuck that noise and shove it where the sun don't shine. You took a bullet for me. I owe you everything. But let's not turn this into some kind of dick-sucking, guy-on-guy Hallmark moment." He slapped Stone on the shoulder and moved past him. Stone had to turn his head away from the reek.

Braxx went over to the driver's side door of the truck and pulled it open, gesturing for Hector to exit the vehicle. "We'll take it from here, amigo."

Hector stared at Braxx as if not quite comprehending his words and then looked over at Stone. "You are letting me go?"

Stone nodded. "You got us inside. We no longer need your assistance. You're free to go."

"What about the truck?"

"Sorry, we still need that," Stone said.

Hector nodded as if that made perfect sense, even though his face showed confusion.

Stone reached into the cab, rummaged through the glovebox, and found a piece of paper and pen. He asked Hector to write down his name and email address, then put the slip of paper in his pocket. "Go home," he said. "If I make it through this day, I'll be in touch and send you some money for all the trouble we caused you." He reached out and put a hand on the man's shoulder. "You may not know it, but you did God's work today."

Hector stared at him, blinking several times. Then he stared down at the two bodies on the ground, flies already buzzing around the pools of gore draining from their bullet-pierced skulls. "This does not look like God's work, *amigo*."

Stone shrugged. "Sometimes God's work isn't pretty."

TWENTY

AS THE DRIVER hightailed it back down the road, Braxx cleaned himself off the best he could using some napkins and a half-empty bottle of water he found in the guard shack, but it didn't do much damn good. The stench filled the cab as he hauled himself into the passenger seat. With the windows down, the morning air managed to seep in and help a little, but not much.

"Not a word," he growled at Stone. "Not one fucking word."

"I've got nothing to say," Stone replied. "You look happier than a pig in shit."

"God, I hate you sometimes."

"Pull your hat down tight and keep your head down as much as possible," Stone said. "We don't want them to see that we're gringos until we're close enough to put a bullet in them."

"Don't fire 'til you see the whites of their eyes, that what you're saying?"

"Something like that, yeah."

Stone shifted the truck into gear and started driving up the path toward the compound. Braxx slumped low in the passenger seat and peered out from beneath the brim of his baseball cap, pulled down as low as he could get it without restricting his line of sight.

After a short distance, the dirt turned to pavement and Stone could not help but wonder how much it cost to have a long, winding driveway blacktopped in the middle of the desert. Then again, this was cartel country, so money really wasn't a problem.

The driveway snaked between two small hills, little more than dunes, covered in sand and creosote brush. As the truck emerged on the other side, Stone and Braxx spotted a large barn up ahead and a hacienda-style mansion a short distance away, a line of black SUVs parked in a semi-circle around a stone fountain. Two guards with assault rifles lounged on the front porch. From this distance, it looked like they were more ready for a siesta than sentry duty.

Stone knew better than to get cocky, but if the guards were this lax and undisciplined, he and Braxx would tear through them like a buzzsaw through toilet paper.

To keep up the ruse that they were just the hog delivery, Stone steered the truck toward the barn, downshifting into a lower gear. As they got closer, they saw the corral full of pigs and the wooden cross just outside the fence.

They also saw what was hanging on the cross.

"Goddamn it," Braxx swore. "That really pisses me off. Tell me we're not letting any of these cartel cocksuckers walk out of here alive."

"You know me better than that," Stone replied. "No mercy, just bullets."

Braxx press-checked his Glock to confirm there was a round nestled in the chamber. "See any sign of the missionaries? Live ones, I mean."

"Could be in the house, could be in the barn, could be

somewhere else. Hell, they could already be dead and gone for all we know. But we're not leaving here until we've searched every inch of this place."

"And killed every motherfucker." Braxx gestured with his chin as two guards stepped out of the barn, cigarettes dangling from mustached lips. "Looks like the welcome party is here."

"Let's say hello."

They both kept their heads down, hat brims blocking their faces, as Stone pulled up next to the hog pen. Before the truck had even come to a complete stop, Braxx opened his door, leaned out, hollered, "Hello, you worthless pig fuckers!" brought his Glock up, and popped two bullets into the nearest guard's chest. The cartel cutthroat went down at the foot of the cross, blood soaking into the dirt, cigarette falling from dead lips to tumble into the dust.

The other guard reacted swifter than anticipated. His FX-05 carbine came up on target before his dead partner even hit the ground. The rifle raked a stream of 5.56mm projectiles across the truck's windshield, punching splintered holes in a zigzagging left-to-right pattern that spewed pulverized glass into the air.

Braxx bailed out of the cab as the rounds slashed the truck. Stone ducked low, feeling the *thud-thud-thud* vibrations of bullets pounding into the headrest. If he'd been a half-second slower to react, his skull would have been turned into a colander. He heard Braxx yelling something —a distraction attempt, most likely—but couldn't see shit.

When the autofire stopped hammering the truck, Stone took a gamble and lifted his head. But he still couldn't see anything, the windshield nothing but a cloudy mess of opaque spiderwebs with holes drilled through them.

He followed Braxx's lead and bailed out of the cab. The door banged hard on its hinges as his boots hit the ground and he immediately dropped into a combat crouch. He pivoted toward the shooter and saw him take a round to the shoulder, presumably from Braxx's gun. The impact swung him around but wasn't enough to make him drop the FX carbine.

The bullet that Stone blasted through his right temple was.

The cartel gunner pitched sideways with his head blown open, blood and brain tissue exploding into the hot desert air.

Stone powered to his feet and turned toward the house, bracing his pistol on the hood of the truck, feeling the heat of the hot metal against his skin. He spotted Braxx ducked behind the corner of the barn. He had no trouble piecing together what had happened. Upon exiting the vehicle, Braxx had dashed for cover, yelling at the gunman to distract him, firing rounds from the Glock in the target's general direction as he ran. One of the slugs had clipped the bastard's shoulder and spun him into Stone's gunsights.

As if to confirm, Braxx saw Stone leaning across the hood of the truck and called out, "Did I get him?"

"You hit him. I finished the job."

"Tag team then, huh?"

"Something like that."

The two guards who had been lounging on the porch of the house ran toward them, one with an AK-47, one with an Uzi, both spitting flame and lead. Bullets tattooed the side of the truck with a sound like rivets punching through sheet metal. One of the captive hogs in the live-stock carrier bellowed out a loud squeal, either protesting the noise or the recipient of an errant round.

The Uzi-wielder stretched out his arm and fired the

submachine gun in a one-handed stance, stitching the barn with 9mm slugs, trying to sink one—or a bunch—into Braxx's flesh. If the missionaries were being held inside the barn, their situation had just become exponentially more dangerous. Wooden walls would do little to stop the fusillade of bullets. Be a damn tragedy to come this far only to have the hostages killed in a crossfire.

As the bullets from the AK-47 tracked across the hood of the truck, zeroing in on Stone's position, he kept his cool and triggered a double tap that took the gunner out of the game. The first bullet split the guy's chin open like a hatchet while the second one impacted slightly higher and smashed into his mouth. He crashed to the ground with his cervical spine shattered and his teeth blown out the gaping, fist-sized hole at the base of his skull.

At the same time, Braxx spun around the corner of the barn, but stayed low, beneath the incoming salvo from the Uzi. He hit the trigger before he was even fully on target, firing rapidly. The first couple of shots from the Glock caught the gunner low, below the belt. He folded over so that the next few rounds punched into the top of his head and pretty much obliterated everything like an eggshell struck by a sledgehammer.

If there were more guards in the house, they chose not to make an appearance. Most likely under orders to remain inside and provide close-quarters protection for Armando Ochoa. In Stone's considerable experience, cartel bosses liked to surround themselves with cannon fodder to soak up the bullets.

"We clear?" Braxx called out.

"For now," Stone replied. "But stay frosty."

"You know me, brother. Ice-cold all the time, unless I'm in bed with the missus."

Stone retrieved the satchel of weapons from the back of the truck and then he and Braxx moved toward the barn door with their guns up and heads on swivels, stepping over or around the men they had killed. As they passed the cross stuck in the ground, Stone paused a moment to look up at Jack Spurgeon's bloody, crucified body. He had not known the young man other than to give a friendly nod in passing when their paths crossed in town, but it still hurt like hell to see him hanging there. Sorrow mixed with rage to form a potent, dangerous cocktail in his soul and Stone vowed vengeance for Spurgeon's horrific death.

Braxx grabbed the handle of the barn door and looked at Stone, who kept his Glock raised and gave him a curt nod. Braxx yanked the door open and immediately brought up his own gun. They ghosted through the entrance, Stone peeling right, Braxx going left, ready for resistance. But none came.

Braxx stationed himself in the open doorway while Stone advanced further into the barn, moving cautiously, stealthily. Just because they couldn't see danger didn't mean it wasn't there. In short time, he found the missionaries locked in the stalls. It took them a few puzzled moments to recognize him but when they did, their fear turned to relief.

"Sheriff Stone?" Bill said. "What are *you* doing here?"

"Long story," Stone replied. "Father Andy will tell you all about it at coffee hour on Sunday, if we make it out of here."

A quick check revealed that Bill and Claudia Dreyson and Gary Gunther looked as good as could be expected, but Dianne Fitzgerald was practically comatose. As Stone set about cutting everyone out of their flex cuffs, Gunther let him know in a hushed whisper what had happened to Dianne.

Stone felt his blood boil and did his best not to elevate his emotions into a blind rage. Fury had its place, but it could also make you foolish and prone to mistakes, and in the kill-zone, mistakes usually got you dead. He also felt a sense of self-loathing that he and Braxx had not shown up sooner. He knew missions took time to plan, to work out the logistics and put all the pieces in place. But while they had been organizing this rescue, Dianne had suffered horribly.

That being said, he knew better than to let the "what-ifs," "maybes," and "could-have-beens" weigh him down too much, at least until the mission was over. Time enough for remorse and reflection later. Yeah, they had located the missionaries and breached the compound, but they still needed to shepherd them to safety.

And take out the sons of bitches who had done this along the way.

Over at the door, Braxx cut loose with a burst of fire from his HK416 carbine. When Stone glanced his way to make sure everything was all right, the warrior shot him a quick thumbs-up and said, "Another dumbass dead in the dirt." He quickly frowned. "Damn. Sorry about the alliteration."

Stone had freed everyone except Amber Lillegard. As he started to search the remaining stalls, Bill Dreyson said, "If you're looking for Amber, she's not here."

"Where is she?"

"They came and took her a little while ago."

Stone felt something cold uncoil in his guts. "Took her where?"

"Up to the house. I heard the guards talking about it."

"For what?"

Dreyson looked pale and stricken. He swallowed hard, a visible lump in his throat, and said, "You know what for."

"Damn it!" Stone snarled, fingers clenching around the handle of the knife he'd been using to cut the hostages free. "Damn it all to hell!" His vehemence star-tled Dreyson, who took a step back as if he no longer recognized the man standing in front of him.

Stone sheathed the knife as he hustled over to Braxx and quickly spelled out the situation for him. "I need to get into that house ASAP. I need you to get the hostages into one of those SUVs and haul ass out of here."

"There could be twenty motherfuckers in that house, each and every one of them looking to put a bullet in you," Braxx protested. "Let me back your play. You know damn well that two guns are better than one."

"You saying I can't handle twenty motherfuckers?"

"That's not what I'm saying and you know it."

"Rescuing the missionaries has always been the prior-ity. If we both go in that house and get ourselves killed, these people will be right back where they started—totally screwed." Stone shook his head. "I can't allow that. Do me this solid, G-Man. Get them the hell out of here."

Braxx clearly didn't like it, but he nodded. "It's your rodeo. I'm just the clown."

"More like the badass bronco that nobody can ride."

"You mean that no *man* can ride," Braxx said with a grin and wink.

Stone peered out the gap in the barn doors, studying the house. "Any guards on the exterior?"

"Negative. After we popped the two on the porch, I haven't seen any other tangos except the one I just dropped, and he came out of nowhere. Just showed up and charged like an idiot. It's complete amateur hour out there."

"I'm sure they have roving patrols, but we'll take that as it comes. I don't have time to go around hunting every jackass running around this place. I need to get into that house and get Amber."

"Let's move to the house together," Braxx said. "We'll take out any resistance we run into and then I'll peel off, grab an SUV, bring it back here to the barn, and exfiltrate with the hostages while you go inside. How's that for a plan?"

"The best kind," Stone replied. "Half-assed and wild as hell."

As Stone grabbed fresh magazines and a pair of grenades from the satchel, Braxx addressed the missionaries, quickly telling them the plan. "So just sit tight and wait here until I get back with the ride, then we'll get the hell outta Dodge."

The missionaries nodded their understanding. Dianne even seemed to be emerging from her trauma-induced catatonia, perhaps sensing that the calvary had arrived.

Claudia Dreyson looked at Stone and said, "You're going to get Amber back, right?"

"God willing," Stone replied. "I promise you that I'll get her back or die trying." *And execute the piece of shit that took her,* he silently added, but figured it best to leave that part unspoken.

Once Braxx had geared up with fresh magazines, they exited the barn in unison, side by side, weapons sweeping, seeking, hunting for targets. They fast footed toward the house at a pace that managed to be both hurried and cautious. Stone's eyes roved in their sockets, scanning all directions, watching for danger from both the front and peripherals. The adrenaline pulsed in his system, but it was controlled and collected, keeping him fueled without pushing him into recklessness. It was a fine line to walk, but he had learned to walk it a long time ago.

He spotted movement at the northwest corner of the house. A cartel gunman leaned out with a Micro-Uzi machine pistol in his hand. A weapon no doubt chosen more for the "cool" factor than accuracy. It stuttered out a stream of 9mm slugs that missed the mark by the proverbial mile, flying well wide of Stone and Braxx's position.

Stone punished the man's poor marksmanship with a rising quick burst from the HK that stitched a line of blood-spurting holes in the man's chest, neck, and face. The Micro-Uzi went sailing from the gunman's grasp as his dead body crashed to the ground.

Braxx spotted danger from above, a shooter positioned in an upstairs window. The cartel soldier broke glass, fired a short, hasty burst that didn't even come close, then pulled back. Without breaking stride, Braxx bracketed the window in his gunsights. When the bastard reappeared for a second try, Braxx sent a pair of bullets chugging through his head. The rifle tumbled out the window and clattered to the ground while the body was punched back inside the house and out of sight.

Stone vaulted up onto the porch. Braxx said, "Good luck, bro," and veered over to the SUVs parked around the stone fountain. He tried the closest one, found the door unlocked, and slid behind the wheel. A moment later the powerful engine rumbled to life. He punched the gas and took off back toward the barn.

Stone watched him go, then plucked a grenade from his pocket, pulled the pin, and rolled it across the porch to settle at the base of the front door. He ducked behind a pillar and waited for the blast.

The detonation blew open the door, literally ripping it off its hinges. Stone immediately tossed a flash-bang through the opening, waited for the thunderous blast of light and noise, and then charged inside. The HK416 was tucked tight to his shoulder and seeking targets.

He spotted a guard immediately in front of him at the base of a wide staircase leading to the second floor of the house. The guy was reeling from the debilitating effects of the flash-bang. Stone dropped him easily with a double tap to the chest, both bullets hitting left of center, drilling into his heart.

He pivoted left and found another target slumped against the wall clutching his ruptured eardrums. Stone ended the bastard's misery with a pair of bullets to the temple that tore away part of his skull.

Stone stayed on the move, sweeping the lower level. He ignored the luxurious furnishings and hyper-focused on possible threats and concealment spots. Another guard appeared from behind the island in the kitchen and Stone took him out with a sustained burst that riddled his chest with red holes. Exit wounds popped open between his shoulder blades and sprayed blood all over the stainless-steel refrigerator behind him.

Stone resisted the urge to call out for Amber. If she somehow managed to answer, it would let him zero in on her location more quickly and precisely, but it would also give up his position to any other guards that remained in the house. Weighing the pros and cons, he opted for silence.

Outside, he heard the sound of an engine revving as Braxx escorted the rest of the missionaries to safety. He heard a burst of gunfire from upstairs and figured a guard was shooting at the escaping SUV from a window. Not that it mattered; anyone with a trained eye could tell the SUVs were armored with aftermarket upgrades that made them bullet-resistant. The idiot upstairs was just wasting ammunition, probably trying to impress his boss.

Ochoa, Stone thought. *The mastermind behind this whole sick operation. I'm coming for your ass, you son of a bitch.*

He performed a tactical magazine exchange, swapping the partially spent mag for a full one, retaining the original on his person for backup, and then started up the staircase. He reached the upper level without incident and discovered a long hallway stretching to the right and left. Each hallway ended at a closed door that Stone guessed would lead into the master suites of the house. The other doors along the hallway would be smaller guestrooms, game rooms, lavatories, and storage closets.

There was a sentry stationed outside the door at the end of the hall to Stone's right. As Stone came into sight, the guard shouldered his AK-47. Stone quickly retreated two steps back down the stairs, taking himself out of the line of fire. A short burst of 7.62mm slugs tore into the landing where Stone had stood a heartbeat ago, blasting apart the terracotta tile and hurling fragments everywhere like shrapnel. He turned his head to shield his eyes and felt a shard graze his forehead, releasing a stream of blood that ran down the right side of his face.

He ignored the painful sting—and the wet heat of the blood—and swung back around the ornate newel post at the top of the stairs. He stayed low, nearly prone, the HK seeking target acquisition on the guard. But the quick-thinking bastard had ducked into an adjacent room. Stone heard him yell, "The *cabron* is upstairs!"

Stone rushed down the hall toward the room but before he got there, he heard a sound behind him. Glancing over his shoulder, he saw another guard emerge from the opposite end of the hallway—probably the same one who had fired at the fleeing SUV—wielding an AK-47 just like his buddy. The cartel goon didn't bother bringing the weapon up to his shoulder. Just fired from the hip, teeth gritted in a menacing snarl.

Stone threw himself to the ground, diving forward and twisting in midair so that he landed on his back. The AK's rounds sizzled above him as he slid across the tiles. He triggered the HK416 carbine as he skidded across the floor, sweeping it through a wide figure-eight pattern designed to saturate the target area with hot lead.

Not every bullet connected, but plenty of them did.

The guard thrashed and shuddered and spasmed under the high-velocity impacts. Blood, flesh, and bone exploded from the ragged wounds as the blistering salvo tore him apart from knees to neck.

Stone slid to a stop right outside the door the first guard had disappeared through. Thinking quickly, he let out a loud, pained groan as if he'd been hit by the burst of AK autofire. A simple ruse, sure, but worth a shot.

It worked.

The door cracked open just enough for the guard to put his eyeball in the gap to check things out. And just enough for Stone to put a bullet through the eyeball.

Staying prone, he reached over and pushed the door open. The room turned out to be a large walk-in storage closet. The guard was sprawled dead with his ass in a mop bucket and the back of his skull splattered all over the shelves of cleaning solutions. Brain matter clung to everything with the sticky tenacity of wet tissue, dripping down like thick oatmeal.

Stone climbed to his feet and faced the door to the master bedroom. He ejected the magazine from the HK, slapped in a fresh one, and then adjusted the sling to shift the carbine to the side as he transitioned to the Glock. He expected whatever came next to be a close-quarters confrontation better suited to a pistol than a rifle.

As he reached for the handle and prepared to breach the room, a horrible scream of agony came from behind the door.

TWENTY-ONE

AMBER SUFFERED—OH, how she suffered—but she refused to let out even a single sob, refused to break, refused to surrender up the broken spirit that Armando 'El Crucificador' Ochoa so desperately seemed to crave like some kind of elixir.

He had beaten her savagely, pummeling her like a butcher trying to tenderize a particularly tough piece of meat. As soon as the guard closed the door behind him, Ochoa had uncinched his robe and let the silk garment slither to the floor to puddle around his feet, standing before her with his thickly muscled, heavily tattooed body on full display. She had nearly panicked at that moment, expecting her violation to happen right then and there.

But to her puzzlement, he remained flaccid, his manhood dangling and unresponsive. As it turned out, he had not removed his robe in order to sexually assault her. At least not yet. No, he had removed his robe simply because he did not want to get blood on it.

She lost track of time as the blows rained down on

her. Seconds? Minutes? Hours? Who knew? Her world became nothing but pain and misery and the endless impact of hard fists. Ochoa tore out chunks of her hair, blackened both her eyes, bruised her face, busted her nose, and pulped her lips. He was a beast, all amped-up rage and unstoppable fury. He pounded on her until sweat lathered his chest, mixing with the blood splatters from her punished body to create a pinkish froth.

Through it all, she refused to cry out. She couldn't stop the occasional involuntary whimper that escaped her pain-clenched teeth and bleeding lips, but that was all she gave the son of a bitch. And clearly, it wasn't enough for him.

He grabbed a handful of hair, his fingernails scraping across her torn scalp, and jerked her head back, raising his fist for what seemed like the thousandth time. "I want to hear you scream, *puta*."

"Never," she wheezed.

"Oh, we'll see about that. I'm just getting started."

The fist crashed into her cheekbone and sent her reeling to the floor. The pain was staggering, like the blow had broken her facial bones. Before she could recover, Ochoa picked her up as easily as someone picks up a torn rag doll and tossed her onto the bed, apparently unconcerned about getting blood on his satin sheets. She tried to resist as he tore at her clothes, but her strength was sapped. He knocked aside her feeble protests as easily as swatting a fly.

But his dick still wasn't hard and ready. Barely even a twitch.

It's a power thing, Amber realized. *That's why he needs me to scream, that's why he needs me to break. He won't be aroused until I'm broken.*

She vowed to die before she let that happen. Maybe she could bite her tongue off and kill herself. She didn't know if that was just a myth or an actual possibility, but it might be worth a try. She would rather bleed out or choke to death on her own blood than suffer the hell Ochoa planned for her.

Her clothes half torn off, Ochoa straddled her waist and began systematically backhanding her face, whipping her head from side to side as his knuckles split open her flesh.

He paused in mid-blow as gunfire sounded from outside.

Brow furrowed, he climbed off the bed and strolled over to the window, using a finger to create a gap in the blinds so he could peer outside. More gunfire could be heard. It sounded like a regular firefight out there.

Amber felt her suicidal thoughts diminish as something close to hope sprang up in her chest. Maybe this was a rescue attempt. Or maybe that was must wishful thinking. Could be nothing more than a rival cartel attacking the compound or bandits trying to snatch the narcotics that were stored here. But she chose to believe it was something better, a slim chance that she—and the others—might get out of here alive. A slender hope at best, but right now it was all she had to cling to.

"Damn it!" Ochoa snarled from the window. "I can't see anything from this angle."

"Maybe you should go out there and check things out yourself," Amber suggested, turning her head and spitting blood onto the pillow. "Instead of hiding in here like a coward, beating up a helpless woman."

Ochoa shot her a scowl and pointed a finger at her. "I'll get back to you in just a *momento*." He marched over to the bedroom door, yanked it open, and bellowed at the guard stationed in the hallway. "What the hell is going on out there?"

"The hog delivery guys," the guard replied. "Word is they rolled up and just started shooting."

"Why would they do that?"

"Unclear at this time, boss. The situation is still developing."

"Let the others handle it. Your only job is to stay right here—right fucking here—and shoot anyone who comes down this hallway."

"You fear *asesinos, señor*?"

"I fear nothing, but there are many people who would like to see me dead. You stay right there, do what you're paid to do, and make sure it doesn't happen. *Comprende?*"

"*Si, señor.*"

Ochoa slammed the door shut, locked it, and turned back toward Amber. A cruel smile creased his lips. If he was worried about the gunfight taking place on his compound, he didn't show it. "Now, where were we?"

He crossed the room with surprising speed for such a big man and was back on top of her in what seemed like an instant. He tore at the rest of her clothes until they were nothing but rags, and his vicious blows moved from her face to other parts of her body as he used her like a living, breathing punching bag. It felt like she was being beat with a sledgehammer, her flesh bruising all the way down to the bone. Even if she lived through this, she would be hurting for weeks, maybe longer.

More gunfire rang out.

Ochoa paused his brutality, head snapping toward the door, eyes narrowed to piercing slits. He held that position for several moments. The blood and sweat ran down his chest in rivulets. An explosion rocked the lower level, quickly followed by another loud bang, which was then followed by even more gunshots.

Ochoa stayed frozen on top of her, waiting to see what happened next. Amber was happy for the respite, however short-lived it might be, and continued to cling to the frayed thread of hope. It was the only thing keeping her sanity intact right now.

A loud burst of autofire from right outside the door startled them both. Seconds later, they heard the guard yell, "The *cabron* is upstairs!"

Ochoa looked down at Amber. There was no fear in his eyes, no concern, no worry. He seemed to take the news that he was under attack in cool, calm, collected stride. "It would appear judgment day is upon me," he said, lips peeling back from his teeth in a cold, wicked grin.

"Good," Amber spat. "You deserve to die, you son of a bitch!"

More gunfire from just outside the door.

"If I am going to die today, you sanctimonious, Jesus-loving whore, then I am going to die on top of your broken body."

He positioned himself to violate her. With shock and horror, Amber realized his manhood had finally risen to the task. Apparently, the thought of taking her while a gunfight—and possibly his imminent death—raged outside his door turned the bastard on.

No! No! No! her panicked mind screamed. *Don't let this happen! Please, God, no!*

Ochoa's hips drew back, preparing for the initial thrust.

In desperation, Amber summoned the final vestiges of strength and surged forward, raising her upper body off the bed, her bleeding face finding the crook of Ochoa's neck. She turned her head slightly until she felt the carotid artery pulsing against her tattered lips. She opened her mouth wide and sank her teeth into his neck, biting down as hard as she could, forcing her teeth through the sweaty skin and rigid muscle like she was trying to chew through a tough piece of steak.

Ochoa bellowed in pain like a bull with its balls in a bear trap and tried to pull away. But Amber clung to him with everything she had, refusing to let go, knowing that if he shook her off now, she would be dead. She bit and ripped and chewed in deeper until, finally, she felt the carotid artery burst between her teeth in a rush of red heat. She thrashed her head to the side like a she-wolf going for the killing stroke, tearing his neck wide open, a dripping chunk of meat caught between her jaws as blood jetted from the mangled wound.

Ochoa screamed in agony.

He rolled off her and climbed to his feet, slapping a hand against the spurting hole in his neck. It didn't do much good; blood kept spraying between his fingers.

He staggered toward the door, leaving a trail of crimson behind him as Amber spat out the hunk of meat in her mouth and let out a roar of primal, triumphant rage.

———

Stone threw himself against the door when he heard the scream of agony, but it was locked. The scream had sounded like a man, but it was high-pitched with pain, so he couldn't be sure.

He holstered the Glock and transitioned back to the HK416. He needed to blow the lock or shoot out the hinges and a burst of 5.56mm rounds would do the job better than .45s fired semi-auto.

He leveled the HK and got ready to go to work.

But before he could pull the trigger, the door swung open.

Stone didn't question his good fortune. Sometimes Lady Luck just showed up at odd times. He hurled himself against the door and felt it connect with something large and solid. He entered the bedroom and saw Amber on the bed, face a battered mess, clothing torn to shreds, teeth bared in a feral snarl. In the next heartbeat, he saw Ochoa reeling against the wall, knocked there by the door, groaning in pain as blood gushed from a ragged wound in his neck. The man's eyes were already starting to glaze.

"Kill him!" Amber screamed, her voice harsh and brittle and raw.

Stone assessed that Armando '*El Crucifacador*' Ochoa no longer posed a threat. With a wound like that, the cartel boss would be dead in ninety seconds, maybe less. Stone lowered the muzzle of the carbine. "The hell with that," he rasped. "A bullet would be a mercy that he doesn't deserve. Let the fucker bleed out."

Ochoa managed to push away from the wall, stumble out the door, and stagger down the hallway. Stone let him go and turned his attention to Amber.

Her clothes were nothing but confetti, so he wrapped her in the silk robe he found on the floor. He kind of expected her to lapse into shock but she stayed lucid, proof of her strength and resilience. As she sat on the edge of the bed and tied a knot in the robe's belt, he saw what he assumed was Ochoa's cell phone on the nightstand and shoved it into his pocket. There was a possibility there would be some damning intel on there that he could feed to Bianca as a way of saying thanks for the help.

"What are you doing here?" Amber asked, swiping the back of her hand across her mouth to get rid of the blood.

"Andy sent me."

She smiled at the mention of her husband's name. "He loves me."

"He damn sure does."

"What about the others?"

"Safe. I brought along an old friend who got them out of here before I came looking for you."

"Safe…" She murmured the word as if it was an illusion, something she would never feel again.

"Come on," Stone said, helping her to her feet. "Let's get you out of here."

They made their way downstairs and out the front door, following the trail of blood left behind by Ochoa. Stone had to give the bastard credit. He had to be one tough son of a bitch to make it this far.

They spotted him over by the hog pen, slumped against a fence post, arms hanging limply by his side. He was still alive, hopelessly clinging to his rapidly draining life.

As Stone guided Amber into one of the SUVs, she said, "Seriously, will you take care of him? He's suffered enough."

"Not in my book."

"Please, Luke, just kill him already."

"You sure?"

Amber nodded.

"Have it your way." Moving fast, with economy of motion, Stone drew the Glock 21 and fired a half-dozen .45 slugs into Ochoa's chest. The series of impacts flipped him over the top rail of the fence, and he splashed down in the mud and pig shit on the other side. The hungry hogs, trained to devour any bodies thrown into the pen, rushed over and started tearing him apart with their sharp teeth, not caring one bit that they were feasting on their former master.

Stone turned away from the sight of flesh being

stripped from bone and climbed into the driver's seat of the SUV. As he pushed the button to start the engine, he glanced at Amber, Ochoa's blood caked on her face. "Thought you were a pacifist?"

"I am," she said softly, her voice wistful, as if aching for something lost.

Stone nodded knowingly. "Let's get you home."

TWENTY-TWO

LIZZY HEARD the drumming all the way out in the Saranac Lake Baptist Church parking lot and smiled. Eric might play contemporary Christian music at the Sunday morning worship services, but when he practiced by himself during the week, like he was now, he typically banged away to secular rock songs. Today it sounded like he was hammering the skins to the tune of *Smells Like Teen Spirit*.

He believes in Heaven, she thought. *But right now, he's got Nirvana on his mind.*

She closed the door of the Jeep Gladiator and locked it. More out of habit than anything else. Saranac Lake was a pretty safe town, and she didn't really expect the vehicle to get boosted in the short time she would be here. She couldn't stay long because her mom needed the Jeep back so she could run out to Luke's and take care of Max and Rocky. But Lizzy didn't need long for Eric to brighten her up. And after suffering through a rough final exam in chemistry, she could use some brightening.

On the good news front, her mom had called to let her know that Stone had texted her and was on his way back from Mexico. Whatever it was that took him there, it seemed like he had been successful and was coming home safe. She didn't know the details and if it had anything to do with Luke's past, Lizzy doubted she ever would. The man had his secrets, that was for sure, and he was remarkably close-mouthed about what he had done before he entered their lives. She had a vague idea, gauged from little things he let slip now and then and from seeing him in action against the various threats they had encountered. But the specifics remained shadowy, murky, like some kind of dangerous creature reluctant to be dragged out into the light for everyone to see.

She walked into the church and the drumming got louder. Her smile grew. Eric was really getting into his music. He seemed in his element behind a kit, and she enjoyed watching him unleash his talent. Stone had told her that there were some people—like David White, for example—that didn't believe drums belonged in church, but that didn't make any sense to her. Why would God give a crap about what kind of instrument someone played?

She entered the sanctuary, recently renovated with a rugged Adirondack motif, and saw him on the left side of the stage. His arms and feet moved in rhythm, hammering out the beat as Kurt Cobain wailed about mosquitoes and libidos. Eric's handsome face broke out in a warm, welcoming grin when he saw her. "Hey!" he shouted over the drums. "Be right with ya!"

She smiled back, nodded, and made her way down the center aisle. His backpack was slung in the corner of the front pew, and she sat down next to it. She tried to ignore the flutters in her heart she felt being around Eric. She hated the thought of becoming one of those girls who got all giddy around their boyfriends.

He finished the song with an extravagant drum

flourish that wasn't part of the original tune and then held both his arms over his head, drumsticks pointed toward the heavens as if worshipping the Lord or simply signifying that he was a badass with the beats. With Eric, it could be either. He was a great guy, but Lizzy had gotten to know him well enough to realize he had a streak of well-concealed arrogance in him. The thought went a long way toward taming those heart flutters.

Don't be judgy, she scolded herself. *It's not like you're some kind of perfect angel all the time.*

He came out from behind the drum kit, used a hand towel to wipe some sweat from his forehead, and then came over to give her a kiss. "Hey, gorgeous," he said after their lips had lingered together for longer than felt right in a church sanctuary.

"Hey, yourself," she said.

He grinned at her. "Thanks for the pictures last night, by the way. I *really* enjoyed them." He gave her a wink. "More than once, if you know what I mean."

Lizzy blushed. "You're so wicked," she said and gave him a stern look. "You *did* delete them, right?"

"Of course. As promised."

"And you deleted them out of your deleted folder, right?"

Eric rolled his eyes. "Yes, dear. This isn't my first time dealing with semi-nude pics, you know."

Lizzy folded her arms, arched her eyebrows, and snapped, "Oh, really?"

"C'mon, don't be like that," Eric said. "You know full well that you're not my first girlfriend."

"Right, and let me guess," Lizzy growled. "Your last one sent you full nudes."

"Well, actually, now that you mention it...yeah. But she was older."

Lizzy knew that feeling jealous about an old flame

was immature, but she couldn't help it. The thought of Eric staring at another woman's naked body sickened her for some reason, no matter how normal it might be.

"I need to hit the bathroom," Eric said.

"Running away from an awkward conversation?" Lizzy taunted, trying to keep her tone light but knowing it came out snarkier than intended.

"Not at all," Eric replied. "We can keep talking about this if it'll make you feel better. Just need to take a piss first."

Lizzy waved him away. "Thanks for sharing. Go on."

"You're not going to run away while I'm gone, are you?"

"Don't worry, I'll be here when you get back."

"Great." He gave her the kind of high-wattage smile designed to melt her defenses and disappeared through a door that would take him to the back part of the church where the bathrooms were located.

As soon as he was out of sight, Lizzy dug into his backpack. Violations of privacy be damned, she was going to check his phone and make sure he had deleted the sexy photos she had foolishly sent him last night. *Never again,* she thought. *What was I thinking?*

She rummaged through his stuff but couldn't find his phone. He must have had it in his pocket and taken it with him to the bathroom.

But in one of the zipped interior pockets of the backpack, she found another phone. It was a much older model than his regular phone, with far fewer features.

A burner? Lizzy thought. *What in the world does he need a second phone for?*

She knew there could be a wide variety of legitimate, above-board, justifiable reasons, but she suspected she knew what he was really doing with it.

It was where he stored the nude—or in her case, semi-nude—photos he received. He could delete them off his primary phone "as promised" and store them on this burner so that no one was the wiser.

Oh, we'll just see about that shit, Lizzy thought.

She remembered the passcode he had given her last night and punched it into the burner, betting it was the same for both phones.

She was right. The screen unlocked.

She clicked on his text messages to see if he had forwarded her texts with the pics attached to this phone.

Instead, she saw texts sent to her mother.

Filthy, perverted, pornographic texts.

She felt something inside of her shrivel up and die, replaced by wrenching betrayal and rising heartache. She looked away from the phone, taking deep breaths, fighting the urge to vomit. A single tear escaped the corner of her eye and trickled a symbolic path of emotional hurt down her cheek. She brushed it away and felt a new feeling joining the conflict roiling inside her.

Anger.

She summoned every bit of control she possessed and by the time Eric returned from the bathroom, she had a pleasant smile plastered on her face. Only very close inspection would have revealed just how brittle that smile was around the edges, and Eric seemed totally oblivious.

He sat down on the pew next to her, slid his arm around her shoulders, leaned in close to her ear, and whispered, "If you're feeling a little wicked, we can make out on a stack of Bibles in the storage closet."

"Sure," she said with bright, false cheeriness. "Sounds like a great idea. Right after you tell me what this is all about." She held up the burner phone with one of the dirty text messages displayed.

Eric seemed caught off guard, but only for a flickering

second. He recovered in a heartbeat. If Lizzy had expected him to at least have the dignity to look guilty, she was disappointed. He just shrugged, removed his arm from around her shoulders, slid away from her, and said, "What do you want to know?"

"What do you think I want to know?" she demanded. "Why are you sending these kinds of disgusting texts to my mom?"

Another shrug. "I've got a thing for older women and I think your mom is smoking hot."

Lizzy stared at him, trying so damned hard not to give him the satisfaction of seeing her cry, but her eyes welled up despite her efforts. "Was it ever real?" she asked. "Any of it? Or did you just use me to get close to my mother?"

Eric stood up so that he was looking down on her, like he was pulling some kind of cheap trick power move. "Listen, Liz," he said. "I think you're a real smoke show, too. The purple streaks in your hair really do it for me, no joke."

"God, you're such an ass."

He continued as if she hadn't spoken. "But I don't want to tell a lie in God's house, so the truth of the matter is, I mostly dated you so that I'd get a chance to be around your mom."

She stood up and faced him, hands clenched together so tight the knuckles turned white. "Are you even sorry?"

"For being attracted to your mom? No."

"For breaking my heart, you bastard."

He grinned crookedly. "That's life, sweetheart."

Her fist shot out, quick and unexpected. She had not always been a fighter, but Stone had taught her some tricks to help her deal with bullies and she used them now. She didn't telegraph the punch so there was no way for Eric to see it coming. Her knuckles sank into his midsection and while he didn't double over, he let out a grunt of pain and took a step back.

She moved forward, closing the gap, not letting him get away, the predator hunting down the prey. A left hook cracked against his jaw, whipping his head around. A right cross whipped it back. Her next shot broke his nose, splattering it from cheek to cheek like a crushed strawberry. He staggered backward another step, a look of shock and pain on his bruised face.

"You are such a fucking asshole," she said, and kicked him as hard as she could right between the legs.

He dropped to the floor clutching his brutalized balls and mewling in agony.

She reached down, grabbed a handful of hair, and jerked his head up so that he was forced to look at her. She was pleased to see genuine fear in his eyes. "If my photos don't get deleted, if they end up on the internet or shared with anyone else, I swear by all that is fucking holy that I'll kill your ass dead and if they ever find the body, it will be in pieces. Do I make myself clear, dipshit?"

She didn't expect an answer, nor did she wait for one. She let go of his hair and his head dropped to the floor with a loud thump that she hoped like hell rattled his brain against his skull. Then she stormed down on the aisle without a backward glance and headed for the door.

Only when she was outside with the sunlight on her face did she start to sob.

TWENTY-THREE

STONE AND BRAXX sat in the Baldwin Parlor annex of St. Luke's Episcopal Church and felt the weariness seep into their bones. They had been riding high on the adrenaline of the mission—the fuel every warrior is familiar with—but now that the kidnapped missionaries had been returned home, the adrenaline was replaced by a tiredness that bordered on exhaustion. They would both sleep for twelve hours straight when they finally got to their beds.

Bianca had grudgingly helped them navigate across the border without hassle, accepting Ochoa's pilfered cell phone as payment. Stone had no problem turning it over to her. He already had what he needed from it.

Stone had used his own funds to charter a private jet to fly them all back to upstate NY. He'd offered to drop Braxx off in Florida along the way, but his friend has insisted on seeing the mission through all the way to the end, which, for him, wasn't until the missionaries were back on home turf.

Andy had wept when Amber collapsed in his arms, both from relief as well as heartbreak from seeing her beaten face and battered body. Pacifist or not, there had been a measure of satisfaction in the priest's eyes when Stone informed him the man who committed the brutality was dead. He left out the grisly details. It was Amber's choice whether or not she wanted to tell her husband that she had torn a man's throat out with her bare teeth.

Bill and Claudia Dreyson had gone home after profusely thanking Stone and Braxx. Gary Gunther was sitting in the hospital with Dianne Fitzgerald, who was still semi-catatonic from the hell she had suffered at Ochoa's hands. Stone had seen plenty of assault victims in his time and suspected she would have a long road back to recovery, and even then, would never be the same.

That was just the way the fallen world worked. Evil could be vanquished, but it never failed to leave behind its mark. Wounds might heal, even mental ones, but scars always remained.

Andy said Jack Spurgeon's family had been notified of his death. They had questions and Andy had promised to give them answers as soon as the facts became clear. They seemed to take some small comfort in the fact that he had died doing the Lord's work.

"Been a hell of a couple of days, huh?" Braxx said, slouched in an oversized armchair.

"That it has," Stone agreed, sitting on the couch in front of the window. The curtains were drawn, shutting out the twilight, and the shadows were deep. A single lamp glowed on a nearby end table. The parlor was an old room and Stone often wondered at the secrets the walls had heard, the confessions the floorboards had been privy to, the whispered sins that permeated the wood and fabric.

"You did a good thing here, Luke."

"We," Stone corrected. "*We* did a good thing. I couldn't have done this without your help."

Braxx snorted. "That's a bunch of crap and we both know it. You could have taken on all those miserable pricks yourself and walked away with nary a scratch."

"Yeah, well, two are better than one, right?"

"You know it, brother. Speaking of which..." Braxx hauled himself up out of the chair. "I need to get home to the wife." He gave Stone a look. "You know, right after I make one last stop."

"You sure you don't mind?"

"It's gonna be my pleasure."

"The jet's on standby at the Lake Clear airport, ready to take you where you need to go." Stone stood up. "I'll give you a lift."

Braxx waved him away. "Relax, I'll take a cab or a horse and buggy or whatever you people use for transportation in this hick town." He reached over and slapped Stone on the shoulder. "You just worry about getting home, saying 'hi' to your dog, and think about giving that Holly chick a call." He winked. "Two are better than one, right?"

"I'll take it under advisement," Stone said. "Now stop playing matchmaker and get the hell out of here. And thanks for taking care of that one last thing."

"No problem. Needs to be done and I'm happy to do it."

Neither of them was big on long, lingering goodbyes. So with a quick shake of hands, Braxx exited out into the cooling air of the summer evening, hung a right at the sidewalk, and disappeared down the street.

Stone watched him walk away and wondered when he would see his friend again. Soon, he hoped, and under better circumstances. God knew they had gone through a whole lot of hell together. Maybe next time they could sit around with beers and fishing poles in their hands instead of guns and knives.

He turned as Father Andy entered the parlor. The priest looked haggard, worn, beat down. Stone could only imagine what the past thirty-six hours had been like for the man.

"How's Amber?" Stone asked.

"As well as can be expected, under the circumstances," Andy replied. "She's in bed, resting."

"She should be in a hospital."

"I know, and I wish she was, but she doesn't want to go. Says she just wants to be home. One of our parishioners is a doctor. I gave him a call and he's going to come over and check on her." He paused, lowering his head to stare at the floor for several long moments. When he lifted it again, there were tears in his eyes. "Thank you for bringing her back to me. I owe you more than I can ever repay."

"You don't owe me anything," Stone replied. "Not a damn thing."

"Not true." Andy shook his head. "You've got blood on your hands because of what I asked you to do."

Stone's mouth tugged up in a wry smile tinged with just the faintest hint of sadness. "Brother, there's barely a corner of the world I haven't killed somebody in. I had blood on my hands long before I met you."

"Maybe, but I can tell it burdens you sometimes," Andy replied. "And I added to that burden."

"Sometimes the wicked need to die in order to protect the innocent," Stone said, "and someone's gotta do the killing. You and I may not see eye to eye on this, but God needs warriors *and* peacemakers."

Andy nodded. "You've got the strength of your convictions, my friend."

"And you've got the strength of yours, even if they're

not the same as mine," Stone replied. "Don't let anyone take that from you." Stone settled his Stetson down on his head. "Now, if you'll excuse me, I'm going home and sleep for sixteen hours straight."

"Lord knows you earned it." Andy reached out and put a hand on Stone's shoulder. "God bless you, my friend."

"He already has," Stone replied. "A hell of a lot more than I deserve."

————

Fifteen minutes later, Stone swung his '78 Chevy Blazer into the driveway of his house. The sun was ball of red fire sinking behind the trees to the west, painting the sky with the kind of radiant, deep-hued colors that only nature can create. Shadows deepened in the tall pines that lined the drive like wooden sentries.

As he emerged from the pine trees and his house came into view, he saw Holly's Jeep Gladiator parked in front of the third bay of the garage. No doubt she was here feeding Max and Rocky and probably hanging around hoping he would come home before she left.

He smiled at the thought of seeing her. Had it really only been yesterday morning he said goodbye to her at the diner? It felt like years had passed since then. The cold ruthlessness that fueled him during the rescue mission ebbed away as he pictured her face, replaced by a warmth that they both, by mutual agreement, continued to deny. Sometimes he wondered why it was so damn hard to break down the walls around hearts that had been hurt before.

Someday you're gonna have to lower the shields, he told himself. *Take a chance and to hell with the risks.*

Holly was sitting at the dining room table when he

walked in, scrolling through her phone while Max flopped at her feet. The Shottie lifted his scarred head in greeting, but that was about it. He let out a huge canine yawn and gave Stone a look that seemed to say, *Oh, you're back. Where ya been, man?*

"Good to see you, too, Max." Stone chuckled.

"Well, *I'm* happy to see you," Holly said as she got out of the chair and walked over, the smile on her face letting Stone know that she felt the same warmth toward him that he did toward her.

God, why does it have to be so damn complicated? It was both a question and a prayer.

"Howdy, cowboy," Holly greeted.

Stone just stood there and stared at her, heart beating.

It doesn't have to be.

"Luke." She looked concerned, the warm smile wilting. "What's wrong?"

"Nothing," he said softly. He reached out, put an arm around her waist, and pulled her close. She let out a little gasp but didn't resist. "Nothing at all."

"Luke, what are you—"

He silenced her with a kiss.

How long they stood there in his dining room, bodies pressed tight, lips melting together, Stone had no idea, and he doubted Holly did either. Time stopped, the world stopped, nothing mattered or remained but the two of them, the silence broken only by the sound of their hearts beating together.

When the kiss finally ended, Holly remained in his embrace, staring up with shimmering eyes. "What was that for?" she asked softly, hopefully.

Stone gazed down at her and called himself a thousand kinds of fool for waiting so long for this moment. "The last woman that kissed me hated my guts," he said. "I wanted a kiss from someone I love."

The word rolled off his lips and felt just right.

Holly's eyes widened. "You...you love me?"

"Yeah." Stone smiled. "That a problem?"

She smiled back. "Not at all, cowboy. Just wondering what took you so damn long."

TWENTY-FOUR

BRAXX MOVED with a stealth that would have made a ninja seem loud by comparison. The carpeted halls of Sacred Impact Mission Group were quiet this time of night, long after working hours had ended. Most of the offices he passed were dark, but light glowed from one up ahead. Somebody working late. The person he had come to see.

Adam Shipman appeared to be in his late thirties with dark, tousled hair and stylish, wireframe glasses opaqued by the reflection from his computer monitor. He had a physique that looked like it got a good weightlifting workout in the gym at least four times a week. Not a power lifter, but enough hard-packed, protein-fueled muscle to keep the slowing metabolism and belly fat at bay. No "dad bod" for this guy.

He looked up with a start when Braxx made his covert presence known by stepping into the office doorway, moving out of the shadows and into the light. "Jeez!" Shipman exclaimed. "You scared the heck out of me."

"Not 'hell' or 'shit' or 'fuck'?" Braxx asked. "The 'heck' is what I scared out of you?"

"Uh, I don't swear. Well, I try not to, anyway," Shipman said. "You know, profanity being a sin and all that." He gestured with his hands at his surroundings. "This is a Christian company, after all."

"Yeah, well, I hear the devil managed to get a foothold here."

Shipman furrowed his brow. "I'm sorry—who are you, again?"

"Name doesn't much matter."

"Well, Mr. 'Man With No Name,' we're closed. So you mind telling me exactly why you're here?"

Braxx's lips skinned back from his teeth in a smile that was anything but pleasant. "Jesus didn't have time to come here and kick your ass, so He sent me instead."

"Doesn't exactly seem fair," Shipman replied. He seemed remarkably calm for a man being threatened with a violence by a stranger. "Seeing as how I haven't done anything wrong."

"Oh, you've done plenty, you son of a bitch." Braxx left the doorway and stepped further into the office. "We know all about your connection to the cartel."

"I don't know what you're talking about."

"More specifically," Braxx continued, ignoring the man's protestation, "your connection to Armando 'The Crucifier' Ochoa. Recently deceased, being turned into pig shit as we speak."

"Now I *really* don't know what you're talking about."

"We have the phone records," Braxx said. "All the texts, the emails, the bank deposits. We even know about your cousin and what you helped her do. All the gory details about how you sold information about missionary groups to Ochoa. Sold out your brothers and sisters in Christ for some filthy silver. You're a fucking modern-day Judas, is what you are, you worthless piece of shit."

The look on Shipman's face made it clear that he knew he was caught, but he remained defiant. He leaned forward, his hands dropping out of sight below the edge of the desk. "If you came here for a confession, you're not going to get one."

"Motherfucker, I can do things to you that would make the devil scream. Make no mistake, you're going to confess everything, and you can bet your ass it won't take me five minutes to get it out of you."

"Too bad you don't have five minutes," Shipman said as his right hand swung into view, gripping a snub-nosed revolver he'd secreted from a desk drawer.

Braxx had been expecting the desperation play. As soon as he saw Shipman's muscles tense for action, Braxx exploded into motion. He moved with the fury and speed of a human cyclone. His left hand swept aside the computer monitor a microsecond before he lunged across the desk with both legs kicking out like dual battering rams. His left boot sent the pistol flying, accompanied by the sharp crack of snapping wrist bone. His right boot smashed into Shipman's chest with enough power to nearly shatter his sternum. Instead, the blow propelled him backward as if he was shot from a missile, the wheels of the office chair skittering across the ergonomic mats on the floor. He crashed up against the back wall with a loud grunt, followed by an agonized howl as the pain from his broken wrist registered.

Braxx was on him in an instant, straddling the man in his chair and going to work with his fists and blade.

Turned out he had been absolutely right.

Shipman confessed everything in less than five minutes.

Braxx rose to his feet and shook the blood from his

knuckles. He had recorded the confession with his phone. He now attached the audio file to a message and sent Stone a short text:

It is finished. Going home.

When that was done, he reached down, grabbed Shipman's head in his hands, and twisted until the bones in the bastard's neck broke apart.

———

Wendy Yates, the secretary for St. Luke's Episcopal Church, looked up from her computer monitor when Stone walked into her office at the Baldwin Parlor annex the next morning. She looked to be in her mid-40s, on the shorter side, with long, straight brown hair just starting to streak with gray. She often dressed like an aging woman trying to cling to the remnants of her youth, with clothing usually out of fashion, if not outright unacceptable, for a woman with more than four decades on earth. Her face was pretty but a smidgen too much makeup worked against the natural beauty God had graced her with.

"Good morning, Pastor Stone," she greeted. She was one of those women who could be super-friendly when it suited her, or downright nasty when it didn't. Stone had heard her sharp, cutting tongue on more than one occasion, though he had never personally been on the receiving end of it.

He suspected that was about to change.

"Morning, Wendy."

"I'm assuming you have a meeting with Father Andy." She jerked a thumb to the right. "He's next door, at the church, either getting ready for morning prayer or fixing a crack in the baptismal, not sure which." She beamed a smile at him, though Stone detected something false and bitter around the edges. "We're all just so thankful you brought Amber and the others home to us, even if poor Amber looks like she's been through a meat grinder." She made a *tsk-tsk* clucking sound with her tongue. "Such a tragedy, losing Jack Spurgeon like that. And what happened to Dianne is absolutely dreadful. I almost feel sorry for whoever did those things, because God is going to judge them something fierce when reckoning day gets here."

"God judges," Stone said. "But sometimes he uses man to do the actual reckoning."

"Interesting theological position," Wendy replied, brow furrowing. "Anyway, like I said, Father Andy is next door."

"I'm not here to see Andy. I'm here to see you."

"Me?" The wrinkles on her brow deepened even more. "Whatever for?"

"You broke the Tenth Commandment."

"What?"

"The one that says not to covet your neighbor's spouse," Stone said. "You fell in love—or at least, lust—with Andy and you decided to have Amber killed so you could try to take her place."

Wendy's lips tightened into a bloodless slash across her face and her eyes narrowed. "That is an *outrageous* accusation," she said. "I have been the secretary at this church for over ten years and have seen at least four priests come and go and my reputation is impeccable."

"Not anymore." Stone pulled out his cell phone. "Your cousin, Adam Shipman, spilled his guts. Word of advice—never trust a traitor. They'll always turn on you in the end." He played the audio recording Braxx had sent him.

Wendy and Stone said nothing as they listened to the confession together and the whole vile, unholy scheme was spelled out. About how Wendy had confided in her cousin that she had fallen for Father Andy. How she wished "that bitch Amber" was dead so she could make a move. How Adam had told her that he could make that happen for her and had even explained the details, how Armando "The Crucifier" Ochoa would take care of everything. How Wendy had strongly urged Amber to go on the mission trip and heartily recommended Sacred Impact Mission Group to handle everything. How she had deliberately delivered the whole missionary team into the hands of a savage psychopath, knowing full well what would happen to them, all because she coveted what she could not have.

When the confession was over, Stone put the phone back in his pocket and stared hard at the woman who had hatched such a murderous, diabolical plan. "That's some real David and Bathsheba shit," he said. "Sending the spouse off to be killed so you can take their place."

Wendy didn't even bother denying the charge. Instead, she injected acid into her voice as she spat, "Are you really going to sit there and judge me, you goddamned hypocrite? Going to sit there and quote the Ten Commandments at me like you haven't broken the sixth one a dozen times since you came to this town?"

"Whatever my sins are, they don't excuse yours. There's a big difference between killing to defend the innocent versus sending people to slaughter so you can take what they have from them. A priest was killed, a young man was crucified, a woman was brutally raped, another woman was beaten within an inch of her life and nearly raped. And all for what? Because you lusted after a married man and coveted that which wasn't yours." Stone felt steely anger flashing from his eyes. "So don't sit there and pretend the things I have done in the name of justice and the things you did in the name of lust are the same damn thing."

"Sin is sin," Wendy sneered. "Isn't that what you holier-than-thou jackasses like to preach?"

"Think what you want," Stone replied. "I'm not here to debate you."

"Let me guess. You're here to put me in cuffs and drag me to jail."

Stone shook his head. "Father Andy doesn't want me to arrest you."

Wendy's face paled. "Andy knows what I did?"

"Andy and Amber both know. I told them everything," Stone confirmed. "All of it."

"And he doesn't want me behind bars?"

Stone shook his head again. "For some reason, no."

"So...what?" Wendy asked. Her eyes suddenly narrowed, but not enough to hide the fear that burst inside them like ruptured balloons. She'd already paled at hearing the revelation that Andy and Amber knew what she had done, but now she paled even more. "Wait, are you...are you going to...kill me?"

"No," Stone said. "I'm not going to kill you."

Wendy looked relieved. "Well, what, then? You're just going to let me walk away?"

"You've got three minutes to get in your car and get out of town," said Stone. "Just drive away and don't look back. Three minutes from now, if I ever see you again, my trigger finger is gonna get real itchy and I'll make you pay for what you did."

"I didn't actually kill those people, you know," Wendy protested.

"Yeah," Stone rasped. "And Pilate didn't actually hammer the nails into Jesus, either."

"That's not fair."

"There's blood on your hands," Stone said. "And you're wasting time. Three minutes. Clock's ticking."

Wendy pushed back her chair, gathered her purse, and left the office without another word. Stone stepped out of the doorway to let her by and then followed her as she exited the front door of the annex. He stood on the sidewalk, arms folded across his chest, Stetson dipped low to block the bright sun creeping over the tops of the nearby buildings, promising a blazing hot day on tap. With hooded eyes, he watched as Wendy climbed into her car and closed the door, her movements fearful and purposeful at the same time. She looked like a condemned woman fleeing their own execution.

Hands on the steering wheel, she glanced over and stared at Stone through the side window.

Their eyes locked for the briefest of moments before the car exploded.

Stone didn't even blink as the vehicle—and Wendy—were engulfed in a hot, roiling ball of flame. She died instantly, which was better than she deserved.

Stone turned and saw Andy standing on the front steps of the church, staring in something close to shock at the twisted, blackened, burning car. He walked over with the flames crackling in his ear and stood next to his friend.

"Thought you said you couldn't do it," Stone said softly, a query in his voice.

Andy seemed mesmerized by the fiery wreckage. "I didn't," he said, his voice even softer than Stone's.

Stone gave him a questioning look. "But I gave you the detonator."

"I left it on the altar. I know I asked you to give me a choice, but in the end, I decided to just let her go and ask God to help me try to forgive her for all the pain she caused. I left the detonator on the altar when I came out to watch her drive away so I wouldn't be tempted to press the button."

"Then who…" Stone started to say, then stopped as Amber shuffled out of the church, her face a swollen, beaten, black and blue horror show.

She stared at the car as the flames continued to devour everything inside. Then she handed Stone the detonator and walked back inside the church without a backward glance.

EPILOGUE

LATE THAT EVENING, Stone sat on his back deck and watched the sun sink behind the tall pine trees that bordered his back field while Rocky munched on some dandelions growing along the fence line. A citronella candle flickered on the table beside him to keep the mosquitoes to ward off mosquitoes and a Jack and Coke, lots of ice, easy on the Jack kept the summer heat from parching his throat. He usually stuck to soda when drinking alone but the events of the last few days had left him feeling like he needed something stronger.

Max was flopped down next to the gas grill, large head resting on his paws, doing what he did best—listening. The look on his scarred but loveable face seemed to say, *Give it to me, man. I'm ready to hear it all. Then maybe you'll give me a damn biscuit.*

Stone sipped his drink and talked to the dog, telling the Shottie everything that had happened.

He found himself wondering how much psychological—and spiritual—damage Amber had done to herself by triggering the detonator that ended Wendy's treacherous life in a blast of fiery vengeance. No matter how she emerged from the other side of her trials and trauma, there was no doubt that she would never be the same person she had been before departing on the mission trip. She had been through hell, and hell changed a person.

He thought about Gerry "G-Man" Braxx and what it meant to have a "ride or die" friend—no, brother—in this world. Someone who would give their life for you without a second thought, someone ready to face hell and highwater with you at the drop of a hat. Too many people never found a bond like that and Stone remained eternally grateful that he had. He could just imagine his buddy's reaction when he told him he had finally taken the plunge with Holly. Braxx would let out a "Hell yeah!" and then remind Stone that he had been a damn fool for waiting so long. And Stone would have no choice but to agree.

Thoughts of Holly made him think about Lizzy. His soul ached for her, for the pain of a broken heart she was experiencing, and not for the first time in her young life. Poor Lizzy had experienced a string of bad luck when it came to boyfriends and matters of the heart and Stone fervently prayed that she would find a guy who treated her with the kind of love and respect a special girl like her deserved.

Stone also intended to have a frank conversation with Eric's dad, man to man, preacher to preacher, so that the good Pastor Wegman would know exactly what his son was up to these days and could hopefully curb the deviant behavior before it spiraled out of control.

He also planned on having an "eat crow" conversation with Deacon White and apologizing for making assumptions and threats. Saying sorry to White—who would be a gloating, insufferable prick during the process —would be about as much fun as taking a power grinder to his back molars without anesthesia, but Stone strongly believed that when you made a mistake, you owned up to it, and when you wronged a man, you owed him an apology.

When he had told Max everything, Stone lapsed into reflective silence. The Shottie seemed to know he no longer needed to listen and rolled onto his side to take a nap, leaving Stone alone with his quiet thoughts.

He knew he would always be a man of duality, caught between two psychological make-ups, the preacher and the warrior forever at odds. But that bothered him less and less these days, the Jekyll and Hyde syndrome giving way to something closer to begrudging acceptance.

Maybe the world didn't need shooters as much as it needed peacemakers...but it still needed them. The scriptures promised a better world down the road, a future kingdom of peaceful perfection, but it wasn't here yet. Humanity had fallen long ago and evil remained to this day. Evil that needed to be fought, evil that needed to be kept at bay, evil that needed to be brought to justice.

It could not be done with whispered prayers and hopes for peace. At least, it could not be done with those things alone. Sometimes evil needed to be met on its own harsh, unforgiving terms, eye for an eye, fire fought with fire. Yeah, the world needed men to fall to their knees in prayer, but it also needed men who got off their knees, grabbed a sword, and prepared to battle the forces of darkness.

Stone struggled to find the balance between saintliness and savagery. Too much of the former left a man closer to God but unwilling to shed blood when necessary, even to protect the innocent; too much of the latter left a man little more than a beast, too far removed from righteousness to temper the bloodshed with sacredness of faith.

"Where does the saint end and the savage begin?" he

wondered aloud, causing Max to jerk out of his slumber and perk his ragged ears back up into listening position. "That's the question."

The Shottie looked at him without offering any answer.

Maybe because he was a dog.

Or maybe, just maybe, because there was no answer to give.

A LOOK AT: THE ASSASSIN'S PRAYER
THE ASSASSINS BOOK ONE

HARD-HITTING ACTION WITH A WHOLE LOT OF HEART.

Burned by the betrayal of his best friend and embittered by the tragic death of his wife, former government assassin Gabriel Asher becomes a freelance gun-for-hire, trying hard to bury the past beneath a violent sea of bullets, blood, and booze.

But some sins refuse to stay buried…

Asher soon finds himself targeted by Black Talon, a brutal kill-team from his past led by the ruthless and legendary Colonel Macklin. Asher just wants to be left alone but when fate thrusts an ex-lover back into his life and she is caught up in the crossfire, Asher unleashes a take-no-prisoners war against his enemies. As the guns thunder and the bodies bite the dust, he finds the scars on his soul being ripped wide open.

With its full-throttle pace, hard-hitting action, and heart-wrenching emotion, The Assassin's Prayer is a relentless tale of redemption for those who know that sometimes bullets speak louder than words.

Publisher's Note: The Assassin's Prayer has been updated with new characters, major revisions, and an exhilarating new ending in this brand-new edition.

AVAILABLE NOW

ABOUT THE AUTHOR

Mark Allen was raised by an ancient clan of ruthless ninjas and now that he has revealed this dark secret, he will most likely be dead by tomorrow for breaking the sacred oath of silence. The ninjas take this stuff very seriously.

When not practicing his shuriken-throwing techniques or browsing flea markets for a new katana, Mark writes action fiction. He prefers his pose to pack a punch, likes his heroes to sport twin Micro-Uzis a la Chuck Norris in Invasion USA, and firmly believes there is no such thing as too many headshots in a novel.

He started writing "guns 'n' guts" (his term for the action genre) at the not-so-tender age of 16 and soon won his first regional short story contest. His debut action novel, The Assassin's Prayer, was optioned by Showtime for a direct-to-cable movie. When that didn't pan out, he published the book on Amazon to great success, moving over 10,000 copies in its first year, thanks to its visceral combination of raw, redemptive drama mixed with unflinching violence.

Mark currently resides in the Adirondack Mountains of upstate New York with a wife who doubts his ninja skills because he's always slicing his fingers while chopping veggies, two daughters who refuse to take tae kwon do, let alone ninjitsu, and enough firepower to ensure that he is never bothered by door-to-door salesmen.